Dicky & The Dame

Bob Able

Copyright © 2024 Bob Able

All rights reserved

This book is dedicated to Andy Crabb, a natural teacher, who generously acted as mentor and proofreader, and dug me out of several holes. A kind and generous friend.

Introduction:-

This story is set in 1963 and although it is a work of fiction, whilst some names have been changed, all the historical context and references are accurate, as far can be reasonably established.

It is astonishing to think that 'conscription', in the form of National Service, bought in after the Second World War, only came to an end in 1963, when the last troops were 'demobbed'. Their service is often forgotten but it is worth revisiting the privations and the danger they faced and the losses they sustained. We owe them a debt of gratitude alongside the 'regular' soldiers, airmen and sailors who actually applied for jobs in the forces of their own free will at that time. Many of the conscripts had to put careers on hold, had family lives disrupted, and several found it hard to get work and reintegrate into civilian life after the upheaval of National Service.

By 1963, in civilian life, the British people generally were able to put the effects of the Second World War behind them, and a great spirit of optimism emerged. Life was improving for ordinary people, as well as the more privileged, in all sorts of ways. It was the start of an exciting era in history.

We follow Richard 'Dicky' Bourne as he leaves the Army behind, but not the effects, friendships and attitudes the era of National Service typified. From watching the building of the Berlin Wall whilst still a soldier, to returning to live with his sister in sleepy suburbia, Dicky's life certainly changes. But before he can settle down and look for a job, he has to find out who the girl involved in the car crash is, and engineer a way to meet her again. But she comes from a social class he could never hope to penetrate, and even in 1963, there are seemingly insurmountable barriers to overcome to launch his career.

Chapter 1

Demob day 1963

The last group of those called up for National Service were assembled for one final parade before their commanding officer, ahead of being released from their duties.

Colonel Reginald 'Tiger' Hampton mounted the small raised dais and prepared to address his men for the last time.

It was an emotional moment. It was the last time the Colonel, or all his military underlings could be rude to the men standing before them, with impunity. But more than that, it marked the end of an era.

'Ahem!' began the Colonel. 'Stand them "at ease", Sergeant Major,' and as the men relaxed a little, he prepared to deliver his last speech to the final intake of National Servicemen.

'Of course,' he began, 'working with a bunch of unwilling, ill-disciplined, lazy, unco-operative, and slow-witted twerps like you was never going to be the sort of commission a military man such as myself would choose, but for Queen and Country, and all that ... Anyway, I shall not detain you long. Some of you have what might loosely be described as "careers" to return to, although reading through the notes earlier, I can't say the life you choose appeals to me much. I accept that we must have farmers and clergymen, I suppose, but some of you rabble seem to be returning to civvy street as book-keepers, lawyers and fiction writers, and even poets. Up to you, of course, how you spend your time, but do we really need those last mentioned? I mean, poets? Ah, well, the world is a very different place now and we all have to adapt to it, I suppose. But I want to leave you with one last thought as you finally walk away. The military life may seem a little constraining to those of you with a literary bent, or maybe the other sort of bent that poets seem to like, but at its heart it turns out good men and true, who are prepared to respect the traditions of honour and service and do their best for their fellow man. Without such men the country we all love would be vulnerable to all sorts of bally nonsense, and before you know it we should have communists and discontent on every street corner. Poets aside, for a moment, I'm sure that is not the sort of England any of us, if we examine our hearts, really want to live in, and the old traditional values must be upheld …'

As he finished, some time later, Private 'Dicky' Bourne blew a quiet raspberry under his breath, and as the parade was dismissed for the last time, he and Private Hamish Swinney made their way back to the barracks to collect their belongs for the journey home.

-oOo-

'What are you going to do first, Hamish?' asked Dicky.

'You mean whan I sober up?' growled the amiable Scot. 'Ah shall have tay visit ma tailor, and get him to take in some of ma trews. I've a waistline now, thanks to all the starvation and running aboot we had tay do in yon camp.'

'Oh, it wasn't really so bad, was it? At least we got three square meals a day and we didn't actually have to shoot anyone.'

'Ah suppose yeh right, but I canna say I'll miss it. What aboot you, young Dicky? Wha does the future look like for you?'

'Oh, I'll get by, I guess. I'm going to try my luck in London, and see if I can get a Literary Agent to take me on, or maybe get a job with a publisher or something.'

'D'ya have anywhere tay live?'

'Not exactly, but my sister said I can sleep at her house for up to a month while I find something more permanent.'

'You'll no consider coming away to the Highlands wi me then? I ken ye said no last time ah asked, but the offer stands, if ye like.'

'That is very kind of you, Hamish, and life in a Scottish castle does sound rather fascinating, but I think I need the hustle and bustle of a London filled with artistic types and that sort of thing around me. I feel I could write something useful in that environment, and things are so different since we went in for National Service. I feel the world is opening up before us.'

'Wheel the offer stands if ye change yer mind, Dicky. I shall miss ye.'

'I'll miss you too, Hamish,' said Dicky, and as they rounded the corner of an accommodation block and stood in the seclusion of its shadow, the two retiring National Servicemen wrapped each other in a not unmanly, back-slapping embrace.

-oOo-

Standing beside the main road outside in drizzle was unpleasant, but essential for Dicky, as he peered hopefully at each black, two-door, Austin A30 that trundled past.

He knew that the only distinguishing mark separating the one he sought from the other, apparently identical, little cars which seemed so prevalent amongst the London traffic, was a stylised, colourful cartoon flower his sister had painted on the boot of her elderly vehicle. But of course, by the time that came into view the car would have passed by.

His only hope was to make himself as conspicuous as he could amongst the stationary and trudging masses on foot, moving in waves like the great herds of Africa, this way and that, on the pavement by the railway station entrance. His sister was not known for her punctuality, it had to be said, but Dicky hoped that on this day of days, as the rain fell a little harder, she would at least make an effort. He hoped his large military-issue kit-bag would also make it easier for his sister to spot him and occasionally he moved it around on the edge of the pavement to ensure it remained visible.

At last with an almost apologetic 'toot' a tired and somewhat faded, black Austin shuddered to a halt beside him. His sister's head, with its blizzard of curls, appeared from within the tiny car.

'Come on then, Richard. I haven't got all day!' she bellowed cheerfully, and indicated that Dicky should use the passenger door, which was facing the traffic rather than the pavement, to manhandle his heavy bag onto the back seat, as the stream of cars and trucks crawled past. Several taxi drivers sounded their horns when having to detour around the door and Dicky's protruding rump, as he struggled to force his kit-bag into the vehicle.

Replacing the folding seat back in an approximation of its original position as it leaned toward the bulging kit-bag, Dicky threw himself into the car and slammed the door.

'It just would rain, wouldn't it, Sophie,' wheezed Dicky above the screech of the windscreen wipers. 'Been lovely all week, but now this!'

'It's the Dicky Bourne luck,' smiled his sister, adjusting her ample frame on the small seat and putting on the trafficator to indicate her intention to edge out into the busy road. 'You bring all sorts of problems wherever you go. You always have.'

'Nice to see you too, Sis,' smiled Dicky, just as a large Bentley, sounding its horn imperiously, crunched into the rear near-side wing of the A30, and following the incident, all forward motion ceased.

-oOo-

'Whatever happened, Jarvis? Will this take long?'

From the back seat of the gleaming Bentley the silvery voice of the only thing more glamorous than the elegant car reached the chauffeur's ears as he began to open the door.

'A little black car got in the way, Miss Camilla, and I'm afraid we have bumped it,' he offered in his best, if somewhat nasal, imitation of the correct modulated speech he had heard on the radio.

'Bumped it? Oh, dear, I hope we are not going to be late. Mother will be at the Savoy by now, waiting.'

'If you will just excuse me a moment, miss. I believe I can soon get them to remove that wreck from our path. High doubt there is much dammidge to speak of.'

But there was damage, and although not severe, there would be paperwork to attend to, no doubt.

Dicky was out of the car in a trice and inspecting the dented rear corner of the Austin and the scratch on the paint above the bumper of the Bentley when Jarvis joined him.

'You could see I was pulling out, I had the trafficator on!' exclaimed Sophie, thrusting herself through the growing crowd of onlookers gathering around the scene.

'She pulled roight aht into 'is path, she did!' observed one of the onlookers, pausing from his duties selling newspapers at the roadside.

'Clumsy kah!' exclaimed another.

'Yon chauffeur 'ad is nose so far in the bloomin' air, 'ee weren't looking where 'ee was goin', few ask me!'

added a passer-by helpfully.

'Snow body 'urt, mind' added a spotty youth in school uniform, who received a sharp tap on the head from the woman who held his hand, for his intervention.

'Come away, young 'Erbert,' said the woman. 'Or there's more where that came from!'

In all the jostling, had it not been for her singular ability to turn heads, Camilla would have been just one more face in the throng. But, though petite, such was the effect of her dazzling personality and immaculate appearance, that a path was cleared for her through the little crowd and she glided, unmolested, to the point of the impact, seemingly effortlessly.

She spoke but one word, but it was enough.

Apart from a 'Coo!' from 'Erbert as he drank in her slim legs under her stylish dress and the wide-brimmed, yellow hat that shaded her large green eyes, the little knot of onlookers fell silent.

'Jarvis?' she said.

-oOo-

Chapter 2

An accidental meeting

Titled ladies, whether they have inherited their status as the daughters of countless Earls, or, as in the present case, by services to the world of film and theatre, always seem to be able to find a good table at the Savoy.

As the sole occupant of the table set for luncheon, just the right distance from its neighbours, Dame Amelia Barron-Zukor sat in splendid isolation toying with a wide-brimmed glass of champagne.

She was becoming impatient.

She glanced at her elegant little gold wristwatch (a final birthday present from her second husband, just before he died) and sighed. Although, when you came right down to it, she had no other pressing appointments, Dame Amelia always gave the impression of being terrifically busy. It had kept film directors on their toes and made mere scriptwriters hurry on with their alterations when progress was delayed on any of the glittering cinematic extravaganzas in which she had appeared. Although all that was now long behind her, the mannerisms she adopted then still made cameo appearances today.

An attentive waiter, standing nearby, misinterpreting the action and imagining this grand lady was in need of his services, hurried to her side to ask if he could be of assistance. She dismissed him with a wave of the slim hand that had once enchanted screen lovers and drawn sighs from enraptured audiences, and glanced once again at her wristwatch.

The waiter caught sight of the large diamond ring on that elegant hand and decided that he was indeed in the presence of some sort of royalty.

'Sorry, Mummy,' said a voice behind him as he moved out of the path of one of his colleagues, directing a trim young woman into the presence of the great lady.

'Camilla! Where on earth have you been?' The unmistakable liquid tones, once so famous and much emulated by several later starlets, gently chided. As the new arrival took her seat, that wonderful voice melted the romantic hearts of the two waiters looking on.

Both had recently seen a rerun of one of Dame Amelia's early films in the 'Golden Days of Cinema' festival held at the flea-pit nearby, in-between their shifts in the dining room.

-oOo-

Dicky wasn't really listening.

Sophie had been talking nonstop, and recounting the little accident from her viewpoint yet again.

'I only hope Gerald doesn't change his mind when he hears about this. I was so looking forward to having a new Mini.'

'New Mini?' said Dicky, taking an interest in this new twist in the tired story of the bump outside the railway station.

'Haven't you been listening, Dicky? I told you. Gerald has promised we can buy a new Mini in time for the winter if we can keep the old car going until then, and if we don't have to spend any money on it in the meantime. Gerald has been promoted and is due to get a bonus from the company, as I was explaining.'

'Sorry, m'yes. That will be very nice. But I've already offered to pay for the repairs …'

'I know you have, and it was very sweet of you. It doesn't matter about the dent on our car, that is just one more for the collection, but it is how much that pompous chauffeur will try to extract for the scratch on the Bentley bumper that worries me.'

The reason Dicky was not really listening was because his head was full of the image of the vision of paradise who had stepped out of the rear of the Bentley and came to stand beside him inspecting the damage. He hadn't be able to think about anything else since.

He had heard the chauffeur call her 'Miss Camilla' as he assured her he would not be long in exchanging names and addresses with Sophie. After arranging to call round to the house when, as he put it, the extent of the "dammidge" had been assessed and a cost estimate prepared, he had guided the lovely girl back into the car.

But it was the smile she gave him as she turned to get into the car that would be haunting Dicky's dreams from now on. She was designed, he decided, precisely to his personal requirements, and was so perfect, it was as though he had drawn up the blueprints for her creation himself.

He had no doubt that she was the best candidate to become his partner in life that he had ever encountered. Dicky did not fall for girls by the dozen like some chaps he knew, but this was actually *it*, he was sure. He just had to figure out a way to get to know her.

'Sophie, why don't you give me the address, and I'll go and see the chauffeur fellow and see if we can come to an arrangement before he turns up with his blasted estimate. If I can square him, Gerald need never know about this little accident.'

'Oh, would you, Dicky? I would be most grateful. You see Petal is getting rather old and I really would love a new Mini.'

'Petal?' asked Dicky.

'Yes, that is her name. From the number-plate … PTL 832 … 'Petal' you see. Silly isn't it, but that is what she has always been called ever since we bought her new at Christmas time in 1952.'

'I see,' chuckled Dicky. His whimsical older sister had always been like this. Her substantial collection of Hornby toy trains each had soppy names and she had christened every one of the model fighter planes Dicky built from kits as they grew up. He remembered 'Daphne', the Lancaster bomber, with particular affection.

'Fair enough,' he said now. 'So can I have that bit of paper with the address, and then I will borrow 'Petal' and pop round to see this Mr Jarvis the chauffeur, to see what I can do.'

'Thank you, Dicky. I put it in my handbag somewhere …' and she began to rifle through the vast Rayon bag with its woven-straw-effect sides in search of the slip of paper that Dicky hoped might just lead to his meeting the girl of his dreams once more.

'Well, that's odd,' Sophie was saying. 'It must be in here somewhere,' and without further ado she upended the substantial bag and shook out its contents onto the dining room table.

But of the note there was no trace.

-oOo-

Although Dicky attended the last ever Demob parade, he was not the last National Serviceman to be demobbed.

That was also in 1963, when Lieutenant Richard Vaughan, who was one of 'No. 277 National Service Intake' left the Army. He briefly commanded the unit Dicky was attached to for the British Army of the Rhine (CPO BAOR) in Monchengladbach, Germany, and stayed on in the Army for a while after his compulsory service ended.

Dicky had never been abroad before, and watching the Berlin Wall being built was an experience he would never forget. Lieutenant Richard Vaughan had taken his squad up the motorway and through the checkpoints, shortly before they left the service, where they saw all the construction work going on. Although many of the men did not understand the political importance of what they were seeing, Dicky felt it deeply. As he came across a newspaper cutting about it, which he discovered when he was unpacking his kitbag later that afternoon, he shuddered at the memory of it.

Somehow it had been arranged that they would be 'demobbed' in England. On the flight back to Gatwick for the demob parade at Devizes barracks the next day, in his civilian clothes, he noticed Lieutenant Richard Vaughan was still in his full uniform and reading the very newspaper cutting he held in his hand now.

The Lieutenant had cast it aside as they landed, and Dicky picked it up as he left the plane and put it in his pocket. As he read it again now, he wondered, not for the first time, about that momentous moment in history and the changes the wall, splitting not just a community but a nation in two, would bring to the world, and what sort of a society would develop as a result.

But the time for conjecture and reflection could come later. He had the keys of the little Austin in his hand and he was going to search it thoroughly for any sign of the slip of paper containing the address, where he was sure the route to his future happiness lay.

-oOo-

Chapter 3

The social divide widens

D ame Amelia Barron-Zukor marched round to the front of the car as they left the Savoy, while Jarvis, as instructed, pointed out the scratch on the paint just above the bumper.

She gave it but a cursory glance, and dismissed it as nothing with a wave of her hand as her daughter, Camilla, spoke.

'There you are, Mummy. I told you we had a bump and that is why I was late. Now perhaps you will believe me.'

The grand Dame glided now through the door of the Bentley that Jarvis held open for her.

'This minor incident is not the point at issue, Camilla,' she purred. 'I was saying that, as ever, you left insufficient time to get to the restaurant, and I was forced to arrive on my own. Had you left earlier we could at least have avoided that.'

'Why was it so bad that you had to go in on your own, Mummy? I'm sure you still made your usual grand entrance.'

'Don't be ridiculous, Camilla. Nobody recognises me anymore. But this was the Savoy, dear. Walking in on your own to dine is simply not done!'

Hiding a snigger, Camilla threw herself down on the wide back seat and clutched one of the loose cushions to her chest as Jarvis closed the door with a respectful click.

'Camilla! Do try to remember deportment! You are not in your no-doubt-nasty little flat with your college friends yet!'

'It's a very nice flat, actually Mummy, as you will see in a minute. And it is certainly not 'little'. It has three bedrooms, two bathrooms and a separate dining room as well as a living room.'

'Drawing room,' corrected Dame Amelia automatically. 'Jarvis has the address, I take it?'

-oOo-

Plans to keep the little car accident from Sophie's husband, Gerald, collapsed before they could be put into action.

Dicky was outside searching the car for the precious

note when Gerald arrived home from work, and of course he immediately spotted the new dent the little car had acquired.

'Hello Dicky, old man,' he had said. 'Welcome home ... What's this? Has Sophie had a bump in the car?'

The tedious explanations which followed forced the search for the all important note to be suspended, of course, and Dicky was obliged to go indoors with Gerald to catch up over tea.

Before he could resume his search, they discussed his offer to pay for the damage, and Sophie explained how matters were left with Jarvis, the chauffeur.

'Well, I call that very good of you, Dicky,' said Gerald, 'and as far as the Austin is concerned, totally unnecessary of course ...'

'But I insist on paying for the damage to the Bentley,' Dicky interrupted. 'If not for collecting me from the station, Sophie wouldn't even have been out in the car ...'

'Well, perhaps not. But she was driving. And whilst I take her point that those old trafficators are not the brightest or most modern form of indicators, the Bentley chappie should have had his wits about him and been looking out for that sort of thing, so he can't be entirely free from blame.'

'But if we must tell the insurance company and

make a claim through them to pay for the damage, won't we lose our 'No Claim Bonus', or whatever it is called, Gerald?' said Sophie. 'And might that not mean it will all work out to be too expensive to buy the new Mini?'

'That is a good point, Sophie, and I know how much you are looking forward to having a new car, but we have to be realistic … If the repairs to the other car are going to be very expensive …'

'It would be a Bentley, wouldn't it …' muttered Sophie.

Dicky drew a deep breath and decided he had to speak.

'Look,' he said. 'This is all jolly unfortunate, I grant you, but I've had a bit of an idea that might help us all.'

Gerald put down his teacup and gave Dicky his full attention.

'Well,' said Dicky, 'I've been thinking that now I'm home and having to look for a job and so on and so forth, I'm going to need some transportation to get around.'

'More lifts?' groaned Sophie.

'Er, no. That is where my idea comes in … How about I buy the old Austin from you, so you will have a bit more to put towards the new Mini …'

'That's an idea,' said Gerald. 'But the trouble with that is it is not worth more than a tenner, I shouldn't imagine, especially in that condition.'

'No, but that is not the point,' resumed Dicky. 'I've already said I'll pay for the damage to the Bentley so you won't have to make an insurance claim to pay for it, so your costs to buy the new Mini won't go up.'

'Well, that is very generous, Dicky,' said Gerald. 'But we don't yet know how much the repairs to the Bentley are going to cost. With that sort of car these things can quickly run to money, and we might have to be realistic and put it through the insurance anyway.'

'Not if we can find the note with the address of the owner on it and I can get round there and square that chauffeur off, before he has time to get an official estimate from a garage. If I can get him to take some cash and avoid all the insurance stuff we are home free.'

'Where is this note, Sophie?' asked Gerald now.

'I can't find it!' wailed Sophie, snatching her handkerchief from her sleeve.

-oOo-

Harry Jarvis was certainly resourceful, if not always entirely trustworthy.

On returning to the sanctuary of Holme Hall, and

the stable block and garages which were used to store the Bentley, and which provided him with his living accommodation as Dame Amelia's chauffeur, he had applied himself with vigour.

A little polish and a lot of elbow grease had completely removed any trace of the recent accident from the gleaming paintwork of the substantial Bentley. It was now as if the event had never happened, and that gave Harry the basis for his plan.

With Rufus Simpkin, the butler, laid up in bed with a heavy cold, Harry had been dispatched with cash to pay the coal merchant.

The task was usually handled by Simpkin in person, because of the merchant's preference for cash, rather than a cheque. This was due, no doubt, to the slightly dubious provenance of the firewood he supplied along with coal and coke to the estate.

The payments were regular and not small, due to the ravenous appetites of Holme Hall for fuel for heating and hot water, and Dame Amelia's assertions that the house was chilly, particularly compared to her previous homes in the United States of America, where she had spent much of her illustrious career.

Holme Hall, in Surrey, had come into her possession and became her home when she married Sir Charles Barron, her last husband and Camilla's father, and retired to England. Although it sat in delightful grounds of several acres, had an ornamental lake, well-tended formal gardens and rather too many rooms for practical purposes, that chilliness persisted and Dame Amelia ploughed money into heating all of it, including the covered swimming pool, perpetually.

Not that there was any shortage of funds to cover this extravagance. Sir Charles Barron and his family had been successful in the City for many years and he left Dame Amelia very comfortably off, which was fortunate, given her propensity to spend money and her taste for the better things in life.

The Estate Manager, a nervous little man named Cyril Bracknell, had reluctantly passed the job of delivering the coal merchant's cash to Harry Jarvis, just as he finished his work on the car, and instructed him to use his bicycle to go into the village and deliver the cash.

As a plan it should have been straightforward and easily executed, but Harry, entrusted with the bulging envelope, arrived a little out of breath and in need of refreshment just as the Horse and Groom opened its doors for the lunchtime trade.

For Harry it was the work of a moment to take up his habitual place at the end of the bar and renew old acquaintances, and it was there that he heard about 'Bumblebee', apparently a 'dead cert' for the 3:00 at Kempton Park.

With assurances that the horse could not fail to take an early lead and come in well ahead of the field, even if it stopped for a refreshing nibble of the turf half way round, Harry finished his drink and called at the bookmaker's next door.

There he met his friend and fellow horse-racing enthusiast, Jimmy, and Jimmy assured him that while 'Bumblebee' was a safety bet for the 3:00, he had had it from the stable cat that 'Wild-Oats' in the 4:00 was quite likely to trounce the field at excellent odds. Jimmy explained that the horse had been quietly training in Ireland, out of the bookmaker's searchlight, and so commanded a generous price as an 'unknown'.

Harry watched as Jimmy placed a substantial bet on the horse, and emboldened by all this talk, and a pint and a half of 'Old Docker' in the Horse and Groom, he reached into his pocket and drew out the envelope of cash.

-oOo-

Camilla opened another window and gave thanks again that her new flat was delightfully cool and bore little resemblance to the stuffy suite she occupied when at home, at Holme Hall.

The rain was but a memory, and the sun shone brightly this afternoon on all of London's hustle and bustle.

Perhaps the traffic noise was something she was going to have to become accustomed to after the quiet of Holme Hall, but that was a small price to pay to have all of London's many attractions spread at her feet, four floors down, and her freedom at last.

At twenty-three, Camilla was not yet entirely financially independent, but she had been able to start drawing an allowance since her twenty-first birthday, which she had carefully saved, at least in part, to pay the deposit and the first three month's rent on her new flat.

When she reached twenty-five she would come into her own money, of course, and at that point she would probably buy a house of her own. But for now the flat, rented from a friend of the family, was giving her a taste of freedom she had never before been able to enjoy, and she was determined to make the best of every moment of it.

She jumped when the doorbell rang, and remembering that she would now have to answer it herself, she skipped to the door to admit a chattering gaggle of her old school friends, and begin the moving in celebrations.

-oOo-

Chapter 4

Looking for answers

Hamish Swinney, on being welcomed back into the bosom of his family at the end of his National Service, had several duties to perform on his estate in the Scottish Highlands.

Swinney Castle, on its little island at the edge of the loch, was almost inhabitable now and the money raised by guided tours and fund-raising over the last fifteen years had gradually improved what was a roofless ruin in 1947. Then his late mother, the widow of the last head of the clan that owned it took over responsibility for it, and with great determination, and not inconsiderable investment, bought it to its present condition.

The family still lived in Drewpin House, five hundred yards from the castle, of course, just as they had for as long as anybody could remember. But the castle was in their blood and its care and restoration, not to mention an intention to eventually derive an income from it as a tourist attraction, ran deep in them all.

Hamish was returning to take on the role of manager of the house, the grounds and the farmsteads they owned in the hinterland of the castle as well as serving as 'custodian' of the castle itself.

He had much to learn, and would be taking on responsibility for organising game shoots, fishing parties, and events; not to mention the guided tours and the maintenance of the land and physical structures of the estate.

Whilst his training for the role had begun, it seemed, when he was a child, he only started the work in earnest when he finished at University. The programme, under his Uncle Jock's careful tutelage was interrupted for two years however, by the call-up for National Service, and now that his uncle was increasingly frail, the pressure on Hamish to step up was growing.

Hamish sat now, in what for generations had been the office of the head of the family, at an elderly oak desk trying to force his mind to concentrate on the account books which seemed to be swimming before his eyes.

He sat back for a moment and glanced around the

room in an effort to re-focus and try again.

The tall bookcases containing great works and a vast array of collected sermons in calf-leather-bound books dominated two walls of the room. On the others, a fireplace and cabinets displaying ancient weaponry and artefacts from the battles fought on this very spot over the centuries, jostled for wall space with hunting trophies and an eclectic mix of stuffed game birds and fish, and the severed heads of everything from stags to a somewhat moth-eaten hippopotamus.

Hamish would have preferred more simple office accommodation to provide less distractions, like the room he occupied while working for the Army Pay Corps in Devizes. That just had a desk, some filing cabinets and a torn map on the wall for decoration. But he would not dare to alter the timeless scene before him now in his Scottish home.

He rubbed his tired eyes, blew his nose, and returned once more to the account books spread out before him. They did not paint an unblemished picture to delight an accountant's eye, and the 'debit' side of the ledger showed appreciably larger numbers than he might have liked.

-oOo-

Harry Jarvis smiled broadly as the results of the 3:00 at Kempton Park arrived on the ticker in the bookmaker's office. 'Bumblebee' had lived up to its billing and romped home in first place, leading the field from first to last.

Harry had returned to the Horse and Groom with Jimmy until the race was run for a further couple of pints of 'Old Docker', and then, having collected their winnings they went back for another visit to await the outcome of the 4:00 race, where 'Wild Oats' carried their hopes and substantial wagers.

At Jimmy's suggestion, Harry agreed that there would be plenty of time to get round to the coal merchant's office and pay their bill when the race was over, but for now they must celebrate the success of 'Bumblebee'.

Thrusting his winnings into the now torn and considerably thinner envelope in his pocket, it did not occur to Harry at that moment to count how much cash he now had in his possession as he revelled with Jimmy and some other acquaintances who joined them in the bar, although the pub was officially closed until the evening.

'Old Docker' is renowned for its abilities to improve the mood of those who try a pint or two at the Horse and Groom, and emboldened by his racing win, Harry had certainly felt those effects fulsomely. By the time he had disposed of his fourth pint, however, he was beginning to have doubts about his ability to keep buying the drinks, and he took himself off to the toilet to count the remaining cash in his envelope.

His win on 'Bumblebee' had been substantial, and the generous odds offered had allowed him to confidently look forward to the results of the 4:00 race. If 'Wild Oats' won he would be very much up on the day. But, now that he counted the money after spending rather liberally at the bar and buying drinks all round, given the size of the bet he had placed on the next race, he discovered that he was currently ten pounds, five shillings and sixpence short to pay the coal merchant. And unless his bet on 'Wild Oats' came good he could not meet his employer's obligations and their reason for sending him out in the first place.

But Jimmy was as effervescent as ever when Harry got back to the bar, and told him to drink up because the results would be in soon at the bookmaker, next door, and then they would be celebrating once more. 'Wild Oats', he insisted, was as sure-fire a tip as he had ever received.

-oOo-

A second search of the handbag and a forensic search of the little old car, inside and out, revealed no trace of the missing note.

'Can't you remember anything about the address, or the name this chauffeur bloke gave you?' asked Gerald, for the third time.

'I told you. All I remember was the address was in Surrey, or perhaps it was Sussex, and some sort of a home, I think.'

'A nursing home, perhaps?'

'That doesn't sound right,' said Dicky. 'The lovely young girl in the back of the Bentley had many years to go before she would be likely to live anywhere like that.'

'So you told us, Dicky. Several times.'

'Think, Dicky. The girl, Camilla, wasn't it … came and stood by you while we looked at the damage,' said Sophie. 'Didn't she say anything?'

'As I said, the only word she uttered was the driver's name … Jarvis, while he wrote out the note leaning on the bonnet of the Austin.'

'Dust!' exclaimed Gerald excitedly. 'His pen might have left a trace in the dust on the bonnet of the car! I saw something like that at the cinema, I think. Or perhaps it was Sherlock Holmes …'

'Holmes! That's it!' cried Sophie. 'Holmes, or rather Holme Hall! I remember now! That was the name of the house, I think.'

'Well done, old girl,' Gerald bit his lip. 'Now all we have got to find is a house called Holme Hall somewhere in Sussex or possibly Surrey, and do it before this Jarvis turns up with his blasted cost estimate. I'm off for a look at that bonnet to see if I can decipher anything amongst all the other scratches.'

'I'm afraid the rain will have washed any dust off, Gerald. But I'll come with you to look,' said Sophie.

'Holme Hall,' thought Dicky, and regretted that Gerald and Sophie were not on the phone, so did not possess telephone directories where one could look things up.

He wondered if the delightful Camilla was on the telephone, and for a moment daydreamed about talking to her using the instrument, 'Jarvis,' she was saying, 'Bring the Bentley round, Dicky and I are lunching at the Savoy.'

The Savoy! … hadn't he heard some jumbled piece of conversation with Jarvis as he got out of the car? Something about her mother being at the Savoy, waiting?

Dicky rushed out to join the others.

'Could I borrow the car to run up to the Savoy, please. I've had an idea!' he announced.

-oOo-

As the bicycle pedal caught him on the fleshy part of the leg for the third time, the yelp which escaped him attracted the policeman's attention as he wobbled past.

As he teetered home, Harry Jarvis had made erratic progress, and now that he could not complete his mission to pay the coal merchant, he was rather regretting the volume of 'Old Docker' he had taken on board.

It took only a short time for Constable Medhurst to read out the notes in his notebook to Mr Cyril Bracknell, the Estate Manager. He had walked Harry the rest of the way back to Holme Hall and after receiving assurances that the senior staff there would now take responsibility for him, was reassured that there was no need to lock him up for the night for being drunk and disorderly.

The tale of woe Harry had told the policeman as they walked was long, and Constable Medhurst could not find it in his heart to bring the full force of the law to bear on the unfortunate man. He had known Harry and Jimmy for several years, and had he met Jimmy earlier in the day, and learned about his tip for 'Wild Oats', he may well have lost money on the horse himself, so he was not without sympathy.

The difficulty arose, of course, when it came to the provenance of the money Harry had used to place his bets, and the fact that it did not belong to him. The question to be answered was whether his employers at Holme Hall, to whom the money belonged, would decide to press charges relating to its misappropriation and the loss of ten pounds, five shillings and sixpence which had occurred.

Cyril Bracknell did not feel qualified to answer that, and it was left that he would put the matter up to the ultimate power, Mr. Simpkin the Butler, in the morning, when Harry had slept it off.

-oOo-

Those at the door for the impromptu house warming had presents for Camilla, and not just bottles of wine, although there were plenty of those as well.

She was presented with cushions, bedside lights, a second-hand 'teas-maid', a string of rather jolly, electric Chinese lanterns, and even an elaborate Moroccan rug.

Her friends spread themselves about the flat and found pop records to put on the radiogram and glasses to pour the drinks, and soon showed no signs of wishing to leave.

Camilla was prepared however. She had filled the large, old, pale-yellow refrigerator with plates of tiny fish paste sandwiches, sausage rolls, bits of celery stuffed with a squeeze of Primula cheese, and chunks of pineapple and cheddar cheese on cocktail sticks stuck all over a grapefruit; and in a cupboard she had the new cheese and onion flavoured Golden Wonder Crisps, not the ones with the blue salt bag, and freshly baked cheese straws, in readiness. After that, she had her showstopper ready and waiting, in the form of her new fondue set, set aside for feeding the little crowd when the time came.

Unlike her mother, Camilla had some rudimentary

culinary skills which she could draw on when the need arose, and although she had asked Mrs Childs, the recently appointed American cook at Holme Hall for some pointers, the fare she was ready to serve now was all her own work.

'Oh, not that "Please, Please Me" Beatles thing again, Annie,' yelled Camilla over the music, as she bought the first plates into the room. 'Can't you find anything else? I've got an Elvis Presley LP over there somewhere … or I've got the new "Summer Holiday" Cliff Richard record…'

-o0o-

'No,' said the doorman. He did not recall a chauffeur called Jarvis delivering a beautiful girl in a grey Bentley. But, by stepping inside the door, and with a little financial inducement, Dicky had more luck with a passing waiter. When reminded of the name 'Camilla' and the approximate time she arrived, he was more forthcoming.

'I think you might mean Dame Amelia Barron-Zukor's daughter. Late she was, and her mother was not pleased. Wonderful voice, the Dame has. Like liquid velvet. Have you seen any of her old films?'

Dicky now had another name. He was getting closer, but his enquiries into where Camilla or her mother lived were not met with further information.

'Heet is not our policy to, ah, dish-up the addresses of hour guests to the strangers,' said a more senior waiter who was passing by. 'Haf chew nothing to do, Bert? Look you are needed on table three ...' and turning his attention to Dicky once more, 'Was there somethink else, sir?'

Dicky moved back into the wide reception area and spotted a row of telephone cabinets. In one of these he found telephone directories and looked up the name Barron-Zukor.

He could find no trace, but then, of course, the directories only covered the London Postal Districts. He knew that Dame Amelia Barron-Zukor lived in Holme Hall in Surrey or Sussex, areas not covered by the available information.

Dicky returned to Sophie and Gerald's house in Pinner disconsolately.

-oOo-

Chapter 5

Money, and where to get it

The problem with 'Old Docker', from the Horse and Groom, is that the impecunious drinker can pay twice for his refreshment, if he overdoes it.

Harry Jarvis was paying the price now.

Having refused the best efforts of Mrs Childs, the cook, and restricted himself to three cups of coffee and most of a boiled egg for his breakfast, he now had to face Mr Simpkin, the butler, and listen to Cyril Bracknell's explanation of the events of the last evening.

Fortunately he would not have to endure their censure and ridicule throughout the entire day because, he remembered with some relief, today was his half day, and at lunchtime he would be at liberty to take his ease.

Even more fortunately his resourcefulness had not failed him overnight, and he had come up with a plan and a story to tell the formidable butler which might save his job and restore the missing ten pounds, five shillings and sixpence to the balance of the cash he had temporarily been holding in trust.

'Cummin 'ere,' said the butler, who was still dealing with his head cold, but was at least back at work now, and indicating the pantry where the interview was to take place. 'How dew hasplain yerself, Harry?'

-oOo-

The morning air was fresh, crisp and clean as Hamish climbed up from the little boat dock to the old castle on its island, and let himself in.

He had not actually had time to visit the structure since his return from Devizes and his National Service, and he was keen to see all the work which had been done since he was last there.

The useable part of the castle itself was not actually very big and could not attract large tours, with about twelve persons at a time being the limit. So an alternative plan had been evolving.

Slowly but surely, the issues with damp and draughts had been, for the most part, dealt with. The new roof now provided shelter across the main building, and the plan was to create a space where families or small parties could have a holiday.

A septic tank had been installed and connected to three bathrooms, one on each floor, and a rather cramped and awkwardly shaped WC with a low ceiling, on the lowest level.

On the top floor, a grand bedroom and dressing room suite had been created and now offered an imposing four-poster bed, shortly to be completed with the addition of a mattress, and a private bathroom accessed through a narrow corridor. Five smaller, plainer bedrooms, currently empty, completed the sleeping accommodation, one floor down.

There was a spacious kitchen and a quite baronial dining room on the lower floor. It had what at first glance, looked like a huge ancient banqueting table but, if you lifted the covers, you could see it was actually constructed from several tables of various vintages screwed roughly together.

A door opened to a broad terrace, once a battlement, with a view out over the loch. It was accessed off one of three uneven stone staircases that ran from the bottom to the top of the imposing building, which, while a little awkward, certainly added to the character of the place.

The other problem in making the castle habitable as somewhere people might choose to spend a holiday, was the lack of natural light. It was built, after all, to be a defensive structure, and little more than holes through which arrows could be fired or slightly larger openings for cannons or buckets of boiling oil to be dispensed were envisaged necessary by its original designers. The interior, with dark stone walls to add to the sense of gloom, was not exactly flooded with sunlight, and it felt oppressive and cold most of the time.

The expensive electric radiators could be used to take the chill off certain areas when the building was occupied, but electricity, for the lights as well as the heating, had to be provided by a large diesel generator, partly hidden in one of the semi-derelict stores on the shore of the little island. Fuel for this machine had to be bought over, in jerry cans, on the wooden boat used to transport tour visitors, so its use had to be carefully planned and rationed to fit in with when visitors came, as well as the weather.

Water was less of a problem because the island had its own well. After many years of neglect, this well had been recommissioned and the water was officially declared safe to drink, although it did look a little brown sometimes when first drawn up through the taps.

Overall, considering what it had been like, Hamish was very pleased with progress. The old castle, or at least the now habitable part of it, was very nearly ready to accept its first holiday guests, and Hamish turned his mind as to how to advertise the accommodation and prepared to seek advice as to what income they could expect.

At last, he thought, there was a way to make a profit from the old building which, it had to be said, had been a drain on the finances of the estate for decades.

Hamish smiled at the diminutive suit of armour which stood under an arch in the hall, and gave it a friendly pat on the head. It had been positioned here to add atmosphere, and was acquired from an architectural salvage yard on the south coast of England. It was not original, having been cheaply made for a film set in the 1940's, but it did add something to the sense of history, if you didn't look too closely.

His uncle was quite right, it was now time to call in the interior decorators, and he was looking forward to the visit, planned for next week, of his old childhood friend and neighbour, Annie Campbell-Manners, to gather her suggestions for decorating and furnishing the rest of the rooms.

-oOo-

It was her mother who encouraged Annie to go in for interior design. It was a fairly natural progression, and she could trade on her grandfather's reputation as one of Scotland's most celebrated architects and the fact that her mother, now retired, still took occasional commissions to decorate the houses of some rather wealthy clients.

At twenty-six and only recently qualified, Annie had yet to break into the world of high-end interior design in her own right, but she was starting to make progress, and had completed a couple of small commissions for friends of her family.

The Campbell-Manners family were firmly established a little more than a mile from Swinney Castle and Dewpin House, where Hamish lived, and as such were pretty much their nearest neighbours. It seemed entirely natural for Hamish to call on Annie to help prepare the castle and he was looking forward to seeing her again.

She could have come yesterday, but cancelled because of a late invitation to a moving-in party. She would be up to the Highlands on Monday, she had said, as soon as she had been to the party and delivered a Moroccan carpet to her friend, for her new flat.

-oOo-

The noise the large whiskey bottle made as he shook out the coins on the bed jangled Harry's delicate nerves, but he was pleased to see that it contained three pounds, three shillings and fivepence. It would be enough to put his plan into action.

'Dew really 'spect me ta believe you about collecting bunny from someone what owes you suffin?' Simpkin, the butler, had asked through his thick cold, in between blowing his nose and coughing.

'Few can't gimme that bunny by the end of this week, we shall hab to see Dame Amelia about it. Oi shan't be serbrised if she don't dismiss you, young Harry.'

With those words ringing in his mind, Harry gathered up his coins, and deciding against the bicycle with a shudder, prepared to walk the two miles from Holme Hall to the railway station at Woodlesham Halt.

He checked that he had the slip of paper containing the address of Mrs Sophie Green in his pocket, and bending painfully, as the movement caused the return of the ache in his head, laced up his boots.

-oOo-

Gerald's newspaper, from the previous evening, had a section advertising 'Situations Vacant', and Sophie pointed out one of the advertisements now.

'Look at this, Dicky,' she called. 'Feldheim and Rosen Publishing are looking for "proofreaders and manuscript submission assessors" at their office in Hatch End, just round the corner from here.'

'Does it say what it pays?' asked Dicky.

'Of course not, but it would give you a start, and it is in the literary world, which is what you wanted, isn't it?'

'What I'd really like is to get commissioned to

write short stories or articles for magazines, Sis. That would allow me to keep body and soul together while I write properly and hopefully find a publisher.'

'Well, how about this then …' Sophie pointed to a block advertisement. 'It says, "Do you have the skills to become a theatre critic, and review new plays and shows in London and regional theatres for an established and respected magazine?" and there is a Box Number to apply to.'

'That sounds more like it!' said Dicky. 'Let me see that advertisement …'

-oOo-

Chapter 6

Progress, of a sort

Dr. Beeching's plan entitled 'The Reshaping Of British Railways', known colloquially as 'Beeching's Axe', involved closing many unprofitable stations and railway lines, and had met with mixed reactions from the voting public. Published in March 1963, his scheme was a constant topic for discussion in the public houses and homes of the population across the nation.

In a few short years the journey Harry Jarvis undertook now would have been far less straightforward and certainly much more expensive, but as things stood he only needed to change trains once to travel from rural Surrey to suburban Middlesex, and seek out the pleasant row of semi-detached houses, built between the wars, where Sophie and Gerald lived, with their house guest, Dicky.

Although the houses all looked very similar, with their faux black beams and white stucco exteriors, it was easy to identify the house in question. The dented rear of the little black Austin, with its stylised flower-petal painted motif was clearly visible, parked on a concrete strip drive in front of the narrow asbestos garage, beside the house.

Harry paused, polished his boots on the backs of his trousers, straightened his tie and drew a deep breath, and then approached the front door and rang the bell.

-oOo-

'Well, you had better come in,' said Sophie, as the dapper little man explained his business.

'Good afternoon,' said Dicky coldly. 'Shall we sit round the dining table?'

With Gerald away at his work, Dicky took on the role of host and offered their guest tea.

'Thanks,' said Harry. 'That would be most welcome.'

As Sophie dispensed the refreshment, with an austere plate of Rich Tea biscuits rather than the home-made flapjacks now cooling in the kitchen, Harry opened negotiations.

'Of course my idea in coming to see you today, Mrs

Green, is to avoid embarrassment to all and see the matter quickly resolved, without a lot of paperwork or insurance company forms.'

'I see,' said Sophie, who didn't see at all.

'What have you in mind?' asked Dicky, noticing how flustered his sister looked and taking charge.

'Well, it's like this, see,' the little man leaned back in his chair and made a sort of steeple with his fingers in what he imagined was a lawyerly gesture. 'When you carelessly swung out in front of the Bentley and caused the collision, like, there was dammidge to both vehicles, of course, but repairs to an expensive motor like a Bentley have to be carefully handled, and that runs to money.'

'Oh dear,' said Sophie, extracting her handkerchief from the sleeve of her blouse.

'How much?' said Dicky raising his hand to silence her. 'What's the damage?'

'Well, that is refreshing,' smirked Harry Jarvis. 'Just the spirit I like to see when opening what could be difficult and protract … eh, lengthy negotiations. I welcome your businesslike attitude, young man. Thirty-five quid.'

'Thirty-five quid!' screeched Sophie. 'It was only a scratch, and it could be said that you were partly to blame too.'

'Yes,' said Dicky. 'I believe the term is "driving without due care and attention", isn't it?'

'Nah, come, come, young man. There is no need to take on.' Harry sat forward in his chair and spread his hands on the table. 'I came in here in a spirit of friendliness and co-operation of my own vol..., of my own free will, to resolve this matter, without no rannygazoo. Not to be insulted and played for a fool. Do you want to agree terms or do we contact the insurance people?'

'Fifteen quid,' said Dicky.

'Thirty, cash down now, and we will consider the matter closed,' snapped back Harry.

'I've only got twenty quid in cash on me,' said Dicky.

Harry sat back in this chair again and drew air over his teeth with a low whistle.

'Well, it seems we have reached an impasse, as they say. To get the Bentley fixed will cost, and I'm prepared to take the risk that it can be done within the figure I mentioned to save you any further embarrassment, but it seems you are proposing to vacil...vac, er, muck about, and cause difficulties for yourselves.'

'What about difficulties for you? What does your employer say about this?' asked Sophie. 'And then there is the damage to the Austin to be taken into account.'

'I enjoy Dame Amelia's complete confidence to resolve the situation and she will leave negotiations entirely in my hands.'

'I bet she doesn't even know you are here …' said Dicky.

Harry looked from face to face. 'Have you got a fiver, Mrs Green? How about twenty-five quid and we call the matter closed?'

'Hey! I'm handling this, Jarvis!' exclaimed Dicky.

Harry allowed one eyebrow to twitch and register distain, but showed no further emotion.

'Have you got a fiver on you, Mrs Green?' he repeated.

'Oh, dear. Very well. Here you are,' sighed Sophie, smoothing the note out on the table. 'That's what is left of the housekeeping. I hope you don't think there is any more where that came from.'

'Very well,' said Harry, holding his hand out towards Dicky. 'I am prepared to take a risk that twenty-five pounds will cover this little difficulty. I'm in danger of making a fool of myself if the repairs cost more than that, but I like your faces and I realise that you are doing your best in these difficult times. So go on then, hand it over.'

Leaving the house and walking briskly round the corner, Harry let out his breath in a long whoosh. It had been close, but he had pulled it off.

Rising from the table, Sophie embraced her brother and thanked him in a broken voice for his efforts.

'Glad to help, Sis,' he replied, and unwound her substantial arms from his neck. 'But excuse me, I'll be back in a moment ...' and with that he was up and out of the door in pursuit of Harry Jarvis. There was something important he had forgotten to clear up.

-oOo-

Following the rigours of National Service, Dicky was fit and could easily outrun an older man if he had to, but fortunately Harry was unaware of his approach and was now dawdling along towards the railway station whistling a popular show tune under his breath. Dicky quickly caught him up.

'Arrrgh!' exclaimed Harry as he felt a hand descend on his shoulder.

'Just one minute, Jarvis, before you make your escape. There is something I need to clear up ...'

'Gawd! I nearly had heart failure!' gasped Harry. 'What do you mean jumping out at folk like that?'

'Sorry, but there is something I must ask you ... Is Holme Hall in Surrey or Sussex?'

'Surrey, near Woodlesham ... Did you scare me half to death just to ask that? What do you want to know for anyway?'

'Well, I ...' Dicky suddenly realised how ridiculous his question must have sounded and found he had no answer ready for Harry's perfectly reasonable response.

'If you are thinking of putting me on your Christmas card list, there is no need to trouble,' said Harry, as it occurred to him that Dicky might try to contact his employer, tell them about the money, and get him into trouble. 'Our bit of business has been quite satisfactorily concluded, wouldn't you say. No need to string it out beyond that, now is there, chum?'

'I'm not your chum, and I bet if I told Dame Amelia Barron-Zukor you had been here and extorted twenty-five quid from us to fix a tiny scratch on her car, she would sack you on the spot.'

'We covered that. Dame Amelia has perfect faith in me to resolve the matter, I told you.'

'Right, just as you say.' Dicky gripped Harry's arm firmly and twisted it up behind his back. 'There is a telephone box over there, and you won't mind if I just put in a call to her and ask then, will you?'

'Ouch! Let me go ...'

'Not a chance.'

Harry felt as if he had been bitten by an alligator, such was the vice-like grip he was held in now.

'Hang on. Let's be reasonable here. I'm sure we can

come to some agreement ...'

'So you don't want me to call your employer then?'

'It's not that ... Dame Amelia is a very busy woman and she won't want to be troubled with trifles like this, and that scratch does have to be fixed, you know. Now let me go!'

Dicky tightened his grip.

'Admit it! You are an adventurer and you came here behind her back!'

'Ow! Gordon Bennett! You are twisting my arm off!'

'Admit it!'

'All right! All right! Arrrg! You'll break my ruddy arm!'

'I'll tell you what,' said Dicky looking menacingly at the squirming Harry. 'If you give me back that fiver from the housekeeping that you forced Mrs Green to give you, and promise never to come anywhere near her, or me, again, I'll let you go. My twenty quid is more than enough to cover that scratch, and seeing as Mrs Green was doing me a favour by picking me up when the accident happened, I have taken responsibility for the matter. There was no need to pinch her housekeeping money as well!'

'Yes, yes. Enough! I'll give you the fiver back if you will just let me go ...'

Still maintaining his grip, Dicky turned so that Harry was trapped up against a garden wall on one side and his iron grasp on the smaller man's arm on the other.

'Get the money out of your pocket with your free hand,' he said in as menacing a voice as he could manage, looking the frightened Harry in the eyes.

'Ouch! Oh please!' begged Harry. 'You can have your fiver. Here, take it!'

Harry reached into the breast pocket of his jacket and drew out the notes he had collected a few minutes earlier, and Dicky pulled a five pound note from the bundle and pushed it into his back pocket.

'Now when I let you go I want to see you run like you have never run before in your life, Jarvis. And know this, if I ever catch sight of you again I will break both your ruddy arms. Are we clear?'

'Oh, God, please!' begged Harry, who was now sweating profusely and beginning to feel quite lightheaded. 'I promise. Yes, sir. I promise. Oh, Ow!'

Pushing him away from the wall, Dicky released his grip, and with a final agonised cry, Harry picked up his feet and ran for all he was worth for the station.

Dicky smiled to himself. That unarmed, hand-to-hand combat training he had received as part of his National Service had never been put to use before, but it had served him well on this occasion.

As he walked back to the house fingering the five pound note in his pocket, he wondered if his sister's housekeeping money would run to sausages for tea.

-oOo-

Chapter 7

A drive out in the country

'And you got the little runt to give you a fiver back too!' exclaimed Gerald as the afternoon's little adventure was explained to him.

'And when I made him see sense, he was glad to do it, given that it was the housekeeping money,' smiled Dicky.

'Well, that's that, and if it had gone to the insurance company we would have had costs too, according to a chap in the office I've been speaking to.'

'How so?' asked Sophie.

'He said there are excess amounts to be paid in the event of a claim, no matter who is to blame. And when I explained what happened to a knowledgeable chap who had been through something similar, he thought it might be that we would lose the case anyway because it would be difficult to prove that it wasn't Sophie's fault.'

'Oh, dear,' said Sophie.

'So I've made a decision, Dicky. You said you might be interested in buying the Austin, didn't you ... so given that you have shelled out twenty quid that we might well have had to pay into the insurance company to resolve the claim, not to mention the increase in our premiums we would face if we lost our 'no claims bonus', I've decided that we can regard the deal as done. Your twenty pounds represents a fair price for our old car, so there you are. It is yours.'

-oOo-

'Right-ho, Annie' said Camilla. 'So we are all set. Tomorrow morning we take the train down to Holme Hall to pick up the two-seater, and tootle off to bonny Scotland for a few days *chez* Campbell-Manners. Sounds like fun to me.'

'You won't mind all the driving, Milly, darling? It is quite a long way.'

'That's all right. It will be the first long run the Midget has had since I bought it nearly a year ago, so it will do it the world of good, I'm sure. Just don't bring too much luggage. The people at MG did not anticipate interior designers needing to use their more diminutive cars.'

Annie laughed at that.

'I'm not proposing to bring any furniture, if that is what you mean, Milly! Just an overnight bag and whatnot.'

'I think this is going to be rather jolly. Tell me again about this Hamish …'

-o0o-

The morning sun was shining, and its bright and welcoming warmth burnished up all of London and its bustling inhabitants as they went about their business. In his sister's suburban nest Dicky had risen early, breakfasted well, and now stood on the front doorstep, taking the air.

But he was too preoccupied to notice the colourful, carefully nurtured flowerbeds, the manicured lawns, and the rows of neatly-trimmed hedges in front of him as he ran through the facts he had gathered in his mind.

He knew that Dame Amelia Barron-Zukor, the owner of the Bentley, lived in Holme Hall, near Woodlesham, in Surrey. Perhaps, he thought, her daughter, the lovely Camilla, who was in the back of the Bentley at the time of the accident, lived there with her.

His eye fell on the little Austin A30, sitting on the narrow drive.

Although to take over ownership he needed to wait until Sophie and Gerald actually bought their new mini, Sophie had agreed that he could borrow the old car when he needed to, as he began to look for a job, and now, opening the creaking door, he sat in the driver's seat and looked around him.

The car had obviously had a hard life. It had been used by Gerald to travel about all over the country for several years when he was just a salesman, before he was promoted and became office based. Externally there were scratches or dents on pretty much every panel, and here and there the paint had faded from the original black to a sort of mottled grey. The stylised flower with its multicoloured petals his sister had painted on the boot was also starting to fade, and actually concealed an unsightly gash the little car had sustained outside a lorry-drivers' cafe where Gerald had stopped for a break many years ago.

Inside, the car had suffered the effects of years of cigarette smoke and the lining of the roof was discoloured and tatty. The little seats were faced in ox-blood-coloured leather, the only optional extra Gerald had allowed himself when the car was first purchased, although now the seat bases were sagging slightly and had cracks in the surfaces here and there. But the engine sounded sprightly enough, despite the milage it had covered, and it rumbled into life now, on the first pull of the starter.

According to the news on the radio in the kitchen as he had his breakfast, the weather outlook was fine, and Dicky decided that what he needed was a run out into the country, so he carefully reversed the car out of the driveway and headed for the Surrey hills.

He had no fixed plan in his mind as to what he would do when he reached Woodlesham, or even if he dared to call at Holme Hall, but he knew roughly the route to take and pointed the little old Austin towards the south.

-oOo-

'Well, I can't say I ain't very surprised indeed that you've done it,' said Mr Simpkin, the butler. 'I dunno how you pulled it off, young Harry, and I hope you ain't been dotting old ladies over the head and pinching their purses or nuffink. But we will let that go for now.'

'So are we all square now, Mr Simpkin?' asked Harry, having handed over exactly ten pounds, five shillings and sixpence.

'Unfortunately there have been expenses to defray,' said the butler, wiping his nose with his handkerchief. 'I had to take a cab up to the coal merchants to pay his bill, as he don't like late payers, and Dame Amelia is a stickler for keeping him sweet ...'

'How much?' asked Harry, with a groan.

'And then there was the beer I had to buy him and Constable Medhurst in the Horse and Groom, by way of an apology ...'

'How much?'

'I should think a crisp fiver would just about cover it, young Harry.'

'And then we are all square and you will forget all about this little incident?' said Harry, producing the five pound note.

'Yes,' said the butler snatching the note and concealing it in a pocket in the recesses of his suit. 'And let this be a lesson to you.'

'Ruddy old thief,' muttered Harry under his breath as he returned to the sanctuary of the garages and his little home in the flat above them.

-o0o-

The village of Woodlesham, in Surrey, was some way from a main road and Dicky got a little lost in some country lanes outside Cranleigh, trying to find it.

It was only sporadically signposted off the main A281 and the village itself was little more than a hamlet.

It boasted a church, a post office and two pubs along a main street, which was punctuated by a war memorial at one end and a railway station at the other. It had half-a-dozen small shops facing a village green and cricket pavilion, but that was about all there was by way of attractions for the visitor.

Driving through the village, Dicky passed a vast Victorian vicarage on his left and then, a mile or so further on, he noticed two tall, brick gateposts, and emerging from a long drive beyond, a blue sports car with the roof down. The car contained two laughing females and sped past him in the opposite direction.

He recognised the driver immediately, of course, and then noticed the sign on one of the gateposts, which read 'Holme Hall'.

-oOo-

Chapter 8

An unexpected visitor

The rain seemed relentless and Hamish sighed as he stared out of the window of the library. He could barely make out the shape of Swinney Castle, five hundred yards away, and the rain seemed to be set in for the day.

On the telephone earlier, Annie Campbell-Manners had told him excitedly that they had reached Penrith where she and her friend were breaking the journey and staying in one of her former college friends digs, before tackling the last stretch up into the Highlands.

Hamish had pointed out that Castle Swinney was still miles on from Glasgow, near Drewpin off the A828, past Ballachulish, and that the last part of the journey could catch people out as it took longer than they might imagine.

Annie had brushed his concerns aside and told him she had worked out that there would be 'good roads', which they would tackle after a night's sleep. She reminded Hamish not to forget that she had done the journey before.

They had already finished the hardest part of the journey, she stated, and had stopped for the first night with friends of her friend, who was doing all the driving, near Coventry. There they went to a party and got to bed just as the sun was coming up. Hamish marvelled at the resilience and energy of his young friend and her driver.

He had asked why they didn't just come on the train, which was, he thought, by far the easiest option. No, Annie had informed him firmly, they had people to visit on the way, and a perfectly good and almost new car to do the journey in.

As the railway line was now scheduled for closure anyway, she would have to get used to doing it by car in the future so this, she said, seemed as good a time as any to follow the route. Annie could not drive herself, but was determined to learn, and as soon as funds allowed, intended to buy a car of her own.

Hamish hoped the road from the A828 was not washed out where it passed beside the loch with all this rain, or the last part of their journey, no matter what sort of a car they were in, would become very difficult indeed.

-oOo-

Two days before, Dicky had witnessed the two girls setting off on their epic journey, but although his own travels were much less ambitious they were not without drama.

Having found the gates of Holme Hall, he had pulled off the road for a moment, and decided to turn round and go back to the little village for refreshment, and if there was a garage, to refill the car with petrol.

He found fuel at a little workshop beside the station and watched two workmen putting up a sign stating that the station and the railway line here was scheduled for closure, as the tank was topped up with the cheaper 'two star' petrol, which the attendant assured him would be fine for the little Austin.

That done, he repaired to the Horse and Groom which had benches outside against the wall and looking over the cricket green, where he was served a reasonably priced pint of a beer called 'Old Docker'.

As he relaxed in the warm sun with his drink Dicky tried to decide what to do next. Should he visit Holme Hall, and if so, on what pretext?

As he sat enjoying his beer, he noticed a large, jolly-looking woman placing buckets outside the Post Office just along the road, and filling them with an assortment of colourful cut flowers. That gave him an idea.

-oOo-

The little Austin crunched busily over the gravel on the long drive and came to a halt beside a sort of roundabout affair, in the middle of a wider section of the driveway.

Dicky reached over to the floor on the passenger side and carefully gathered up the large bouquet of fresh flowers. His purchase had delighted the sub-postmistress who had served him, and he hoped they would be well received now.

Only rarely had the sub-postmistress been able to make up proper bouquets, using the flowers she grew in her garden at the rear of the shop. But she had excelled herself on this occasion and produced a floral tribute every bit as good as you might find in a much grander establishment. As she handed it over, she thought the flower arranging classes she had attended with the local W.I. had served her very well, and she was proud of the display.

Dicky opened the creaking door of the car with his spare hand now, and pushed it wide open with his foot. Being careful not to catch the flowers on the edges of the door opening, he climbed out and gently kicked the door shut as he approached Holme Hall, with some trepidation.

His approach had obviously been noticed, as before

he could ring the bell, the door opened wide, and a very grand and imposing old fashioned butler said 'Tradesmen and deliveries rand the back.'

'Er, no, I don't think you understand,' Dicky began to explain. 'I have come to see Miss Camilla Barron-Zukor to... er... pay my respects.'

'Miss Camilla is not at home,' said the butler imperiously, but behind him Dicky noticed movement.

In a diaphanous gown, an elegant and upright older lady was gliding across the hallway.

'Who is it, Simpkin?' she purred.

'What name?' said the butler, and then repeated Dicky's name to the grand lady who was now approaching.

'What beautiful flowers,' she said. 'Are they for me?'

'The gentleman says he has come to pay a call on Miss Camilla, madam.'

'Then Camilla has missed a treat.'

'Very good, madam,' said the butler, stepping to one side to allow his employer to approach.

'Was my daughter expecting you?' she asked. 'If so I must apologise. She has unfortunately forgotten your appointment and driven off to Scotland with her friend.'

'Oh, well I …' spluttered Dicky.

'Amelia Barron-Zukor,' said Dame Amelia, offering a slim and beautifully manicured hand 'I don't think we have met …'

Dicky took the hand and did his best to smile winningly.

'I'm terribly sorry that you have had a wasted journey, and I must say Camilla has been very rude dashing off and not even leaving you a message. The least I can do is offer you some tea and apologise. Although I have to say that she told me she would be away for a week, so those lovely flowers will not survive until her return.'

'Well, in that case, would you like the flowers, Dame Amelia?' said Dicky. 'It would be a shame to see them go to waste.'

'You charming boy! What a lovely gesture,' fluttered Dame Amelia. 'Take the flowers and put them in water, Simpkin. And you will join me for some tea, won't you, young man?'

'Well, that is very kind of you,' smiled Dicky, as the butler gathered the bouquet from his arms.

-oOo-

Tea, Dame Amelia decided, was to be taken in the library today and despite the warm weather Dicky was surprised to see the embers of a fire burning in the substantial grate.

'Now, tell me, Richard ... I'm sorry, you said to call you Dicky, didn't you ... do you work?'

Dicky explained that his National Service had just come to an end, so he was currently looking for employment.

'What line of work would interest you?' enquired his hostess in her wonderfully modulated and once very famous voice.

Dicky explained that he hoped to work in something to do with the literary world, and when she enquired further, blushing profusely, he explained that he had written two unpublished plays and had sold several short stories to various magazines.

'And is that how you met my daughter?' asked Dame Amelia, offering Dicky the plate of sandwiches for the second time. 'I do like to see people with a good appetite. In my previous life everybody of your age always seemed to be trying to starve themselves half to death.'

'Your previous life?' asked Dicky.

'Well, it was before your time, of course,' she smiled, 'but I was in pics ... that is to say films, you know. Out in America mostly. Acting a bit. The camera can put on weight, hence all the dieting.'

'Gosh!' said Dicky. 'That must have been fascinating.

I have always had this idea of writing for cinema one day …'

'You must show me some of your work … the plays, I mean. I still know one or two people in that business who might be interested …'

'Well, I …'

'Funny that Camilla has not mentioned you before, Dicky. Especially as she would know I would be interested in how you make your living. Have you known her long, and how did you say you met her?'

So far, of course, Dicky had not said how he met Camilla or explained that he hadn't really met her properly at all, but now he drew a deep breath and explained about the car accident and their meeting, such as it was.

'And you called just because you were concerned to establish that she had suffered no ill effects? How utterly charming!'

'Well, I …'

'And bought flowers as well! Perhaps I got too used to American manners, or the lack of them, in the years I spent there,' said Dame Amelia. 'But one could not expect such courtesies from American youth. Delightful, quite delightful!'

Smiling, Dame Amelia offered Dicky the sandwiches for a third time.

'And such a pity that you missed Camilla. It is like something out of a Greek Tragedy ... but it occurs to me that we can do something about it.'

'I beg your pardon?' said Dicky.

'These plays, my dear boy ... what are they about?'

-oOo-

Harry Jarvis, in his shirtsleeves, had just finished cleaning the interior and polishing all the woodwork in the Bentley until it glowed, and thought he had earned the cigarette he lit now.

Inhaling deeply, he straightened up and began to stroll across the courtyard, and towards a spot where the sun illuminated a patch of grass and a section of the old wall, on which he liked to lean when taking his ease.

Glancing towards the house, he gave a start, dropped his cigarette and stopped in his tracks.

There, on the drive, right outside the front door, stood a battered Austin A30, with an unmistakable hand-painted flower motif on the boot.

-oOo-

'And send Jarvis to me, would you, Simpkin?' said Dame Amelia as the young man was shown out.

-oOo-

Chapter 9

Communications

As he turned out of the gates of Holme Hall, Dicky felt marvellous.

By a series of what seemed to be miracles, he had not only met Camilla's mother but secured her interest in reading his plays. And who knew where that might lead?

Of course he had not seen Camilla herself again, which was a pity. But Dame Amelia had said that when she had read the plays, and when her daughter returned, she would write to him with a view to inviting him down for what she called 'a visit'.

He set off for home in a happy reverie, and managed to find his way through the tangle of lanes without getting lost.

As he closed the door of his sister's house, she smiled

and pointed to the dining table.

'A letter came for you,' she said.

-oOo-

'Come in,' called Dame Amelia. 'Ah, Jarvis, there you are.'

'I .. I .. I .. Dame Amelia, I can ...'

'Yes, yes, Jarvis. But please will you explain how this accident involving my daughter happened.'

'Well, it was like this ... That beaten-up old car was picking up outside the station, and then she, Mrs Green, I mean, just pulled out in front of us.'

'And were you going very fast?'

'Oh, no, ma'am. We was crawling along in 'eavy traffic, like ...'

'And was there much damage?'

'Not to the Bentley, ma'am, no. A slight scratch only. An' I polished it right aht.'

'And to the other car?'

'That old banger had so many dents on it, it was 'ard to say which was new and which it 'ad before.'

'But there was a dent?'

Harry twisted his fingers together and looked at his shoes. Here it comes, he thought. She is going to sack me, and probably expects me to pay for the repairs to that grotty old car as well.

'Yes, ma'am,' he replied sheepishly.

-oOo-

Dicky picked up the letter. The envelope was typewritten and it looked official.

'It's not going to open itself, Dicky,' laughed Sophie. 'Would you like a paper knife?'

'I wonder …' said Dicky as he slid a finger beneath the flap and opened it. 'I hope it's not a bill.'

-oOo-

'Quite charming, and such a lovely gesture, to bring Camilla flowers like that.'

Harry wasn't really sure he was following what Dame Amelia was saying. He had gathered that the driver of the old Austin had called for tea, which must mean she knew him, he supposed. But other than ascertaining that nobody was hurt in the accident, she had not asked him any further questions about it, and now seemed to be talking about enjoying her visitor's company.

Then he remembered that this same young man had threatened to call Dame Amelia from a telephone box, and his arm still ached from the encounter.

Now he thought perhaps he really did know her, and

actually had her telephone number. His confusion grew as Dame Amelia seemed to be prattling on about him being a playwright or some such, and how she was expecting him to come for a visit.

'So the least I can do is to get you to run up to town to pick him up, Jarvis, when the date is set. That will save him having to rely on that old car of his for the journey.'

Remembering what this same young man had said he would do to him if he ever saw him again, Harry Jarvis shuddered.

Now Dame Amelia seemed to have run down and had nothing else to add, and was looking at him as if expecting a response.

'Yes ma'am,' he said, trying to control the slight tremble in his voice. 'Will that be all?'

As he left the library he was certain, beyond any shadow of a doubt, that what he needed now above all else, was a pint of 'Old Docker', to soothe his shattered nerves.

-oOo-

Sigsmund Publications had offices in High Holborn, according to the piece of their headed notepaper, which Dicky now held in his hand.

What was more, they explained that they owned the titles 'Theatre and Cinema News', incorporating

'Box Office', and 'The Critical Review' and in response to his application, were prepared to offer him an interview to be considered for the post of 'correspondent' for the above named publications.

The details of the work would be explained to him at the interview, the letter said, but would involve quite extensive travel in and around London and the suburbs, so his own transport would be required.

The letter went on to give an interview date and asked him to telephone their offices to confirm that he could attend.

Those offices would be closed now, but Dicky resolved to be at the telephone box at the end of the road to call them at half past nine in the morning, when they reopened for business, without fail. He had already counted the coins in his pocket for the telephone, so was ready to the last button to make this most important call.

-oOo-

'And so we have got to wait for the AA motorbike,' said Annie. 'And I'm running out of coins so will call you again later. Bye.'

Hamish supposed he should not have been surprised. It was a very long way from Surrey to the Scottish Highlands, and although Annie had explained that her friend ... Milly, wasn't it ... had a new car, and they had broken the journey into sections, neither of them seemed to be capable of fixing the flat tyre they discovered as they made to leave the place where they had spent the night.

They were still at Annie's old college friend's digs, near Penrith, which fortunately had access to a pay telephone. Better that this happened there, than miles out in the country, on some deserted road in the wind and rain, he thought.

-oOo-

As they sat down to dinner that evening, there was animated talk about what happened when Sophie had met Gerald as he was coming home from the office, at the railway station, and they went together to the car dealership on the High Street.

'Yes,' said Sophie excitedly. 'It is a Morris Mini Minor Super De-Luxe in pale blue with a cream coloured roof.'

'Two tone, eh? And it is brand new?' asked Dicky.

'Yes, of course, and it will be arriving at the garage on the High Street on Tuesday.'

'So you haven't seen it yet then?'

'No,' said Gerald. 'But when we went in and asked about new minis, the chap there told us about this one coming in, and Sophie fell for the colour scheme, of course.'

'I did rather,' Sophie twittered. 'They had a red one there for sale, but it wasn't a Super DeLuxe, so it didn't have things like opening rear windows and …'

'The red one was a bit cheaper, mind you,' interrupted Gerald. 'But Sophie had set her heart on that blue one.'

'You wait until you see it, Dickie. It's so pretty!'

'Well, you have only seen a picture in a pamphlet so far, old girl. When you see it in the flesh you might not like it so much,' said Gerald.

'Oh, I know I shall, and I can't wait.'

'Well, assuming all is well, Dicky, could you take Sophie to the garage on Tuesday afternoon, when I'm at work, and then on to the Post Office to do the paperwork, do you think?'

'No problem, Gerald. I should be delighted.'

'Then we can get the Austin changed over to your name. Perhaps the garage can sort out doing the test on it at the same time. It will be due in a fortnight.'

The old Austin was due to have one of the relatively new Ministry of Transport roadworthiness tests, introduced a couple of years ago, that applied to all cars over ten years of age. Dicky was hoping it was going to pass without extra garage bills to pay. Even taking the test cost fifteen shillings, and soon he would have to take out insurance to drive it on his own account as well, so costs were mounting up.

'Petal will pass her examination, I'm sure,' said

Sophie. 'She had her first ten year test last year and the man in the workshop said something about her being quite solid underneath, so I'm sure there is nothing to worry about.'

But Dicky was nevertheless a little concerned. If he got the job with Sigsmund Publications he would be needing reliable transport, although quite where he would have to travel was not yet clear. No doubt all would be revealed at his interview, and following his telephone conversation this morning, that was now fixed up for tomorrow.'

-oOo-

Chapter 10

Arrivals

It only took twenty minutes or so for the AA Patrol to find Camilla and Annie, and a little less than that for him to change the problem wheel for the spare.

What did take time, however, was firstly an attempt to mend the puncture, and then the replacement of the tyre with a new one in the greasy car repair workshop not half a mile from the digs where they had spent the night.

Before giving it up as a bad job, the mechanics there spent over an hour attempting to mend the puncture, although afterwards, as they drove away with a new tyre fitted, Annie did make the point that the oily mechanics were obviously just stringing the job out so that they could chat up two pretty girls.

'Revolting,' said Camilla. 'Both of them.'

'The salesman chap we saw first was quite dishy though, don't you think?' replied Annie. 'I wish I had learned to drive and could afford a new Ford Anglia, like that one he was polishing. But climbing Mount Everest would be easier for me than saving up the five hundred and eighty-nine pounds he wanted.'

'And he said the price was going up in July,' added Milly, shaking her head.

On that point of agreement, they continued on their way to Scotland.

-oOo-

The Army insisted on reports on everything, which fortunately for Dicky meant that he had learned to type and even to take shorthand whilst in their service.

As everything that was typed then had to be filed, Dicky was kept busy when working in the Pay Corps. offices. But not so busy that he had not found time to type out one top copy and two carbons of both of his plays.

One of the carbon copies of each was now in a large brown paper parcel, packed with a hand-written note, on the dining room table ready to be taken to the Post Office and sent through the mail. He would take the parcel in as he passed on his way to the offices of Sigsmund Publications in Dane Street, High Holborn.

Although not usually troubled with nerves, Dicky noticed that his hand was shaking slightly as he gathered up the parcel and prepared to leave the house. One can never be entirely comfortable about the prospect of a job interview, and Dicky, if asked, would have compared it to waiting to see the dentist.

Depositing the parcel, and the drive to High Holborn, went off without a hitch, and Dicky found what appeared to be the last available parking space in Red Lion Square, just a few steps from Dane Street, and the offices he sought.

As he parked the little Austin behind a rather grand Daimler, he noticed a man in uniform with a pronounced limp, approaching.

The yellow band around his cap announced in capital letters that this was a Traffic Warden. One of the group, formed in the last couple of years, that prowled the streets of Westminster issuing fines to those parking illegally.

'Excuse me, Officer,' said Dicky, stepping from the car. 'Am I all right to park here?'

'Are you delivering, or planning on making a long stay, sir?' replied the immaculately turned-out individual, snapping smartly to attention.

'Oh, ah,' said Dicky. 'Well that rather depends on what you mean by a long stay. I am here for a job interview.'

'Well,' said the Warden, relaxing a little on his heels, 'I see. Is the interview to take place far from here?'

'Oh, no, just down there, in Dane Street. Sigsmund Publications. I'm hoping to get a job as a theatre critic.'

'Are you now? Sigsmund Publications, you say. I hope you don't mind me asking, but don't they publish 'Theatre and Cinema News?'

'I believe they do, as a matter of fact, why do you ask?'

'Mrs Bacon is greatly addicted to the cinema, you see. And we subscribe to that periodical. We also occasionally take 'The Critical Review', which I believe is also one of theirs.'

'Well, that is a coincidence. As I understand it I shall be doing reviews for both those titles, if I get the job, and having to tour about, going to theatres and cinemas all over the place.'

'I think then, for the purposes of the exercise, we can regard your parking here as falling under the heading of "deliveries", in the circumstances,' smiled the Traffic Warden. 'And may I take the liberty of wishing you every success at your interview.'

'Thank you very much, Mr Bacon, wasn't it?'

'Ernest Bacon,' said the Warden holding out his

hand. 'Always a pleasure to meet people from the world of Cinema and Theatre.'

As Dicky shook his hand, he admitted that he could not claim to be so connected yet, but explained that, having just returned from National Service he did need the job.

'Army man?' asked Ernest.

'Yes, as it happens. I was in Monchengladbach, Germany until recently.'

'Good heavens!' exclaimed Ernest. 'I was there myself until four years ago. Retired as a 'Regular'. What rank did you hold, and what did you do?'

'Oh, only a Private, you know,' said Dicky, who had never had any ambitions to progress through the ranks during his National Service. 'I finished up working in the Pay Corps.'

'Pay Corps? Well I never! Me too, at least at the end of my time. Sergeant Bacon it was back then, based in Devizes when we came back to Blighty.'

'Devizes! That's where I was demobbed!'

'Well, what a small world it is, and no mistake!' and the two men shook hands again.

'How did you end up doing this?' asked Dicky.

'Well, I'm quite close to retirement age, you see, and it is pretty difficult for old sweats, I mean ex-soldiers, like me to find work, especially given ...' He indicated his left leg.

'Injured?'

'Blown up. When I was with the Bomb Disposal boys. It doesn't trouble me too much now, so long as I keep exercising it. That's how I ended up in the Pay Corps.'

'I'm sorry to hear that, Sergeant, but I'm glad to see you got a job.'

'Thank you very much, young man. And can I wish you all the best for your interview. Mrs Bacon and I will look forward to seeing your name in print in one of those journals.'

With mutual expressions of goodwill, and after the kindly Traffic Warden had promised to keep an eye on the Austin, Dicky took his leave and crossed the road towards the offices of Sigsmund Publications.

-oOo-

'Well, the flars was for Miss Camilla, as I understand it, young Harry.' Simpkin, the butler, put down the silver salver he was polishing. 'Can't say for certain if Camilla dunt know him, mind.'

'Well, she didn't seem to know him when we 'ad the accident,' said Harry, scratching his chin. 'But that *was* the old Austin I bumped on the drive, sure as eggs is eggs.'

'Seems rummy to me,' said Mrs Childs, the cook, as

she lifted the teapot. 'More tea?'

'Not for me, Mrs C,' said Harry. 'I've got to take the old duck shopping up town, and better watch how much I has to drink.'

'Nowhere to stop and take a whizz, you mean?'

'Keep it clean,' said the butler disdainfully. He did not approve of the forthright manner of speaking Americans employed, and always checked Mrs Childs when she slipped into the vernacular.

-oOo-

Hamish finished his drink and was making ready to turn in for the night when the telephone rang in the hall.

'Hullo?' he said grabbing the instrument. 'Who's there?'

'It's me, Hamish,' Annie's voice sounded tired, 'We are here at last.'

'Wha time d'ye call this? Ye should ha been hame hours ago!'

'Och! Don't you start, laddie. We just got a bit lost is all.'

'Lost?'

'Mebbe I need a wee bit more practice map reading.'

'I was worried sick!'

'Oh, were you? That's sweet, Hamish,' giggled Annie. 'I just called to say we will meet you up at the castle at eleven in the morning, if that is OK?'

'Eleven? Can you no' make it earlier? Say nine?'

'No! We will not say nine! Milly is fair worn to a splinter after all that driving. I've just put her to bed.'

'Oh. Eleven then.'

'Yes, Hamish. Eleven. We will see you then.'

-oOo-

Chapter 11

'It's not what you know, it's who ...'

'Cynthia, how many times have I told you to knock!' exclaimed Samuel P. Sigsmund, proprietor of Sigsmund Publications, hastily picking up a glass containing a golf ball from the carpet and concealing a putter behind a bookcase.

'Sorry, Mr S. That bloke's 'ere, wot you wanted to call for a nintervoo.'

'Tell him to wait where he is, then tell Captain Wilson to step in. He will conduct the interview as I will be leaving for the weekend shortly, after the introductions.'

'Right you are, Mr S.'

'And Cynthia, bring us tea would you.'

'Tea? Yes orright, Mr S. Will do.'

'And biscuits.'

'And biscuits, just as you say, Mr S,' and with that, Cynthia withdrew.

-oOo-

Dicky heard the exchange recorded above quite clearly, because Cynthia had forgotten to close the door behind her, so he knew what to expect.

'You're ta wait 'ere,' announced Cynthia, returning to the visitors' area, before she bustled off down a corridor, presumably to make the promised tea.

Resuming his seat in the waiting area, Dicky took a moment to take in his surroundings.

The office, on the third floor, was served by an old-fashioned lift with folding concertina gates which clanked and groaned, as if it was all too much trouble.

The ground glass in the door facing him as he left the lift proclaimed that he had arrived at the offices of Sigsmund Publications and that this door was for the use of 'Visitors'.

As the butterflies in his stomach cranked up the tempo and attempted a determined tango, Dicky had to take a deep breath before he opened the door.

The waiting area was windowless and slightly stuffy, but otherwise unremarkable. It was furnished with a small desk and what appeared to be a collection of old dining chairs. There was also a coffee table, liberally scattered with previous editions of the various publications which began life here.

Other than a large ornately-framed hunting scene, the arch leading to the corridor through which Cynthia had scuttled, and three identical doors, the tobacco stained walls were unrelieved.

He was greeted by the redoubtable Cynthia as he entered, and if you have been paying attention you will already know what happened immediately after that.

-oOo-

'Would you care to step through, please,' said Cynthia, and Dicky was admitted to a large and comfortably furnished office where, when he could not avoid it, Samuel P Sigsmund spent his working life.

Samuel P was standing behind an imposing desk now, smiling and holding out his hand.

'Mr ... ah ... Bourne, how do you do,' he said.

The pudgy hand Dicky now grasped belonged to a short, almost circular man with a strawberry complexion, and a protruding stomach, stretching the buttons of an uncomfortable-looking suit jacket that appeared to be two sizes too small.

As he introduced himself, another internal door opened to admit a tall elegantly dressed man with a fine white moustache and an upright, military bearing.

'Ah, Captain Wilson,' said Samuel P. 'You will have to excuse me, Mr Bourne, I cannot stay long. But Captain Wilson will be conducting the interview ...'

'Edward Wilson,' said the newcomer in a bold and self-assured baritone, clasping Dicky's hand in firm grip. 'Pleasure to meet you.'

-oOo-

Fifty minutes later, Dicky was once again in Red Lion Square, walking towards the little Austin.

Noting with relief that there was no parking ticket on the windscreen, Dicky lit a rather pleased cigarette, jumped in and drove around three sides of the square hoping to catch a glimpse of Sergeant Bacon, the kindly traffic warden, to share the joyful news about his new job.

His meeting with the traffic warden, and then that which took place with Captain Edward Wilson during his interview, had cemented in his mind that there were considerable advantages to be had from his recent National Service, which whilst not initially obvious, had certainly helped him now.

Samuel P Sigsmund had stayed long enough to drink

a cup of tea and eat three of the five biscuits on the plate, before taking his leave. The interview was then conducted in the friendliest of terms by Captain Edward Wilson, who was most interested to discuss Dicky's recent military history, and added a little of his own story to the conversation.

'Yes, Guards initially, but then transferred to join the chaps in Germany. You were with the 277 National Service Intake, I see from your letter. Looks like we both spent time in Monchengladbach, where I had my first command.'

Dicky found the coincidence very much to his advantage as the interview progressed, and digressing from the main agenda for a moment, they discussed the privations of the accommodation the army used in Germany and specifically in Monchengladbach.

'Well, thank goodness all that is behind us,' smiled Edward Wilson. 'Now, where were we?'

The interview proceeded on these cordial lines, and as they parted Dicky was pleased to hear that an offer of employment would be encapsulated in a letter shortly, and Sigsmund Publications looked forward to him joining their organisation.

On leaving, Dicky could find no trace of his favourite traffic warden and had to bottle up his excitement until he got home and could tell Gerald and Sophie.

-oOo-

On the long car journey to Scotland, the conversation had inevitably covered many topics, but a theme had developed around music, and particularly certain bands.

'I don't know much about Scottish music,' Camilla had confessed. 'I've heard of 'The Dormobiles' of course, and everyone knows all about Johnathan, but I don't really like his miserable ballads. I prefer something with a bit of zip and ginger.'

'Well, 'Fleetmaster' are a bit more heavy rocky, you might like them. And if you like more middle-of-the road stuff, there is always 'The Grinders'. But have you heard of 'Heather and the Heartaches? I went to school with most of them.'

Whilst 'Heather and the Heartaches' had an interchangeable line up of hopeful, would-be musicians at school, Heather, whose real name was Heather, and Siobhan who preferred to be called Moira because, she claimed, nobody could spell Siobhan, were the constant factors.

At school, the two friends had been good at music, with Moira featuring in several school band concerts playing instruments as diverse as the violin and the harp, while Heather could sing. Really sing.

Heather's was not an operatic or classical style of delivery, but rather an earthy, slightly unhappy-sounding voice, that was nevertheless robust enough to fill a room. It was ideal for country ballads or the sort of sad lyrics where the singer had to inject the impression of being on the brink of tears.

Heather and Moira worked hard to create a song in the school breaks which, perhaps unsurprisingly, given the timbre of that voice, was called 'Crying on Her Pillow'. When they thought it was ready, they performed it for their music teacher during a lunch-hour. It turned out to be the start of something big.

Heather's voice was accompanied initially by a modern, bluesy, slightly rocky melody played on the violin, or fiddle, as she preferred to call it, by Moira.

After they had captured the music teacher's interest, a piano, electric bass and guitar were added to the ensemble, and with occasional assistance from the music teacher herself on drums, 'The Heartaches' took on a more complete sound.

The piano was played by Angela Grey, who had studied the instrument almost since birth, and been encouraged, or should that be 'pushed', by her parents to enter and win several competitions. She had become quite accomplished. Although she could play anything put in front of her, in any style, and could inject the appropriate feeling into her playing, when it was carefully explained to her what emotion was required, she was not an imaginative musician. Heather and Moira called her 'Angela the Automaton' in that cruel way schoolgirls will, although they were happy enough to have her in their band.

The electric bass, with the instrument initially borrowed from the music teacher, was played by Ally, as he was known, who had been christened Alistair. His was a melancholy face, even when happy. He just looked soulful, or thoughtful perhaps, all the time. But he could hold a tune and produce inventive rhythms from the instrument that soon had feet tapping.

The guitarist was almost painfully shy, but he was good. Gareth, known as Gary, had moved with his parents from Wales when he was turning fourteen, and had not grown up with the others in their school. Having joined at that awkward age, he was always something of an outsider. He had an attractive face with deep brown eyes that were almost black, and Heather and Moira both fancied him, although he was much too shy to chat them up.

He took comfort in his guitar and his dedication enabled him to play virtually anything, but he was addicted to blues music'. So much so that he once scandalised the school Chaplin by asking if his God would mind if he worshipped Muddy Waters instead.

Now that school was behind them, but still with the assistance and contacts of the music teacher, 'Heather and the Heartaches', as they were now known, got a record contract and released 'Crying on Her Pillow' to critical acclaim. They followed it with a selection of 'covers' and a couple of original songs.

Whilst those new records did not grab the attention of the first recording, they did float about in the 'Top 100' for a while and enabled them to find a permanent drummer and buy Ally a bass guitar of his own. After that, they embarked on a couple of tours and started to make a name for themselves in and around the Scottish clubs.

'I still keep in touch with them,' announced Annie. 'Mebbe I can get tickets to a gig if they are playing nearby.'

-oOo-

Chapter 12

New beginnings

The First Class postman had excelled himself and Dicky had his job-offer letter in his hand by mid-morning.

Attached to the letter there was a hand-written note from Captain E. Wilson, asking him to telephone the office on receipt so that the 'trial period' mentioned in the letter could be discussed and dealt with.

Dicky almost ran to the telephone box on the corner of the road to make the call.

-oOo-

At shortly after eleven, as they rounded the corner, the castle came into view.

Although the weather was still gloomy, the effect of the imposing building on its little island in the loch, surrounded by swirling mist, was certainly atmospheric.

'Wow!' said Camilla. 'Well, there is no mistaking that, is there? I take it we have arrived.'

'Yes,' said Annie. 'Take the next turning left, up that lane by that gate; it leads to the house. We will meet up with Hamish there and walk over to the castle.'

'I thought you said you have to go on a boat?'

'You do, but it is only a few yards really, and Hamish will walk us down to the boat and take us over.'

As the house, which was their initial destination, came into view around a stand of trees, Camilla noticed that it was a mishmash of styles and had obviously been much extended over the years.

'So the family live in that house, not the castle, then?'

'Yes, didn't I explain that? Although the castle looks huge from here, quite a bit of it is a ruin, and the bit they have been making habitable is really only eight or nine rooms. The idea is to let it out for events and holidays.'

'I see,' said Camilla, as the car crunched along a rough gravel section of the narrow lane. 'What sort of events do they have here?'

'Well, nothing at the moment. That is why we are here. Hamish wants me to look at the possibilities to decorate and furnish it for a selection of uses, and maybe we will discuss what sort of events could be held there.'

'With all that grass sloping down to the little island,' said Camilla, who could now see the main part of the loch and the water separating the castle from the field they were driving beside, 'it would make a smashing venue for a summer concert.'

'How do you mean?' asked Annie.

'An open-air sort of thing with the musicians playing on the island and the customers sitting on the grass and picnicking perhaps.'

'I'm not sure I understand,' said Annie.

'I went to something like that in 1961, in Richmond Athletic Ground. I think it was called the National Jazz Festival. They had all sorts of bands there and charged two pounds a head. You could bring a picnic if you liked, and it was quite a relaxed affair.'

'I heard something about that, now you come to mention it. Who took you there?'

'Do you remember Giles Pendlebury? His father owns a London Club and was something to do with organising it, so we got in for free.'

'You never went on a date with Giles Pendlebury! We used to call him 'The Pimply Pustule from Pimlico Road'. A horrid little slimy oik if I remember correctly.'

'He was rather, but free tickets to a music concert were quite tempting. Perhaps you could do something like that here, maybe showing off Scottish bands.'

'You know, that's a jolly good idea, Milly. I'll put it to Hamish.'

-oOo-

Once the call had connected, Dicky had to shovel money into the box as he waited for Captain Wilson to come to the telephone. He hoped he had enough coins.

'So', said his future employer, after the initial pleasantries. 'We think we would like to see how you get on with a simple sort of test.'

'Oh?' said Dicky.

'Yes, and if that turns out well I think we can dispense with any more of this "trial period" stuff and regard your appointment as fixed.'

'What sort of test?' asked Dicky nervously.

'Nothing too onerous, old chap, don't panic. We just thought it might be an idea if we sent you to review a film which was recently released, so we can see the sort of copy you can produce.'

'I see,' said Dicky, who wasn't sure he did see.

'Yes, an easy job, actually. What we thought was to ask you to toddle over to Croydon and write us a review of 'A Sweeter Taste', a film they are showing there from tomorrow evening. It started life as a play and has now been made into a film.'

'I see,' said Dicky again, who was beginning to get the picture.

'It is a very modern sort of thing, as I understand it, but I'm sure you will soon get the idea. If you get your copy over to me the next morning that will be fine.'

'Will you be printing it in one of the magazines?' asked Dicky.

'What, for a film like that? I shouldn't think so. But it will serve us well to see what you can do, we feel.'

'Right-ho,' said Dicky. 'Where does this screening take place?'

-oOo-

'Right,' said Sophie, as Dicky, returning from the telephone box, closed the front door behind him. 'Are you ready to go and see the Mini?'

'Oh, ah. Yes, right-ho, Sis,' said Dicky. In all the excitement he had put the much anticipated trip to see the blue-and-white Mini to the back of his mind.

'I'll get my coat then.' Sophie opened the cupboard

under the stairs and selected a light coat. 'There is just one thing ...'

'How do you mean?'

Sophie hesitated with the coat in one hand and the handle of the cupboard in the other.

'Well, I know Gerald said we could do it, but it is rather a lot more money than a standard Mini, and it will eat up all of the bonus Gerald will be getting and then some. Am I being a bit selfish, do you think, Dicky?'

It was difficult to know how to answer that.

If he was honest with himself, Dicky had to confess, that when the idea of getting this car was first discussed, he struggled with the concept of buying it based on its colour scheme. He also thought that the purchase of a brand-new car was a bit extravagant. But he had to set that against the fact that he could not afford a new car, and Gerald and Sophie could.

Of course, being Sophie, she was very excited about a new car and that was understandable. She had gone without the use of a car for many years while Gerald used the little Austin to tour around as a salesman, and it was only since he was promoted and became office-based, that the car became available for her use.

As so often happens, though, once she became

accustomed to the convenience a car provided, she now saw it as an essential.

And then of course there were the neighbours to be considered.

Walking along the road, Dicky had noticed various new or newish cars parked in the driveways of each of the almost identical houses. He had seen a brand new Vauxhall Viva being polished, and assorted, quite modern Fords outside the houses along the road. They were all obviously the proud possessions of the upwardly mobile homeowners in this part of Pinner. Perhaps, he thought, the cars provided a point of difference, to make one aspirational householder appear more successful than the next. He had no time for that sort of petty snobbery himself, but he could see how, living in this suburban environment, it might affect his sister.

Amongst such a display of new and expensive machinery, the little Austin did appear somewhat down-at-heel, although he personally admired its durability and perversely regarded its battered body and faded paint as a sign of having fought the good fight and won through. It deserved respect, to Dicky's way of thinking.

'Well, that blue-and-white Mini will certainly stand out amongst the other cars in the road,' he said, as tactfully as he could. 'You will be the toast of the neighbourhood.'

'Blue-and-cream,' corrected Sophie automatically. 'But even so …'

'Well, let's go and look at it, Sis. Then you can decide,' smiled Dicky. 'Who knows? You might not like it when you see the real thing.'

-oOo-

Harry drove the Bentley into the courtyard with its little collection of buildings in front of what was originally the 'carriage house', where it lived. His little flat, approached up a wooden staircase beside the big car's resting place, beckoned.

After Harrods, Dame Amelia had taken tea at the Dorchester, and then went back to visit Harvey Nicholls. During this time Harry had to wait in the car and occasionally be prepared to move it if delivery vehicles needed to use the various entrances and service roads he had learned he could briefly stop in, when visiting these places.

Each time they arrived at a new venue, he was instructed as to how much time, in minutes, Dame Amelia required until he was expected to pick her up at the main entrance, with all due ceremony. She became quite cross if he was late or if, for whatever reason, she could not make an elegant exit, so he had to get it right.

In the meantime he had to dodge about, finding corners in which to tuck the Bentley to wait until she was ready for him to pick her up.

Sometimes, where they knew him, it was all right. At the Dorchester, for example, he could pull into a small yard reserved for deliveries and visit the kitchens, where he was usually rewarded with a cup of tea, and sometimes a bun, if he was lucky.

But trying to find anywhere to park near Harvey Nicholls or Harrods was always much harder work, and he sometimes had to keep driving up and down Knightsbridge while his employer visited the stores. Today she visited the area twice, with a break at the Dorchester in between, so Harry had to find places to stop there on two separate occasions.

These excursions could be exhausting, and although it was early, as soon as he had run a chamois leather over the car, Harry was looking forward to his supper and bed.

But rest and repose was to be denied him for a while longer as Mr Simpkin, the butler, was standing in the courtyard beckoning to him.

'You are to take the old duck up Piccadilly for ha' pass eight. She is going to 'The Pigalle Club', or some such name, to meet 'Erbert Walters for supper.' Harry groaned as the butler let out a little wistful sigh.

'I 'ad high 'opes for the Dame and this Walters,' he said. 'Used to see a lot of 'im she did. Aways off dancing and that. Its 'im wot produces those plays up west. She was in one of them ... years ago it was.

Can't remember what it was called now.'

'You mean Sir Herbert Walters, the theatre impresario?' asked Harry, impressed.

'That's the chappie. So, young Harry, you 'ad better smarten yourself up and get ready fer a long night. They used to stay out dancing till all hours, they did.'

-oOo-

Chapter 13

Fresh ideas

Drewpin House had windows on all sides and Hamish had seen the little blue MG Midget approaching long before it reached the front door. As a result he was ready, with the door open, when they pulled up.

With the introductions over and offers of tea politely refused, Hamish announced that they should put on stout footwear and he would take them down to the castle.

Annie was prepared and had picked up her old walking boots before leaving her family home. But Camilla had nothing suitable with her, so Annie had put a pair of her mother's wellingtons in the little MG, explaining that the grass might be wet after all that rain.

The wellingtons were two sizes too big, but at least they stopped Camilla ruining her expensive city shoes as they sloshed down to the loch through the wet grass, and for that she was very grateful.

Now that they were close, the castle seemed enormous and quite forbidding. As Hamish helped them into the wooden boat, which stank of spilled diesel fuel, the towering building blocked out what sunlight there was, and sent a shiver down Camilla's back.

'Not cold, are you, Milly?' asked Annie.

'I'm fine,' she replied. 'Just a little overwhelmed by the size of the castle, I guess.'

'Ah wish it was as big as it looks from this angle,' said Hamish. 'Most of it is a ruin now, ye ken, so it looks big, but only a fraction can actually be used.'

'Most of it fell down a couple of hundred years ago,' added Annie. 'But I'm sure we can make something out of the bit that is left.'

'Aye, and get it so we can make some money outta the wretched thing,' said Hamish.

-oOo-

Sophie loved the blue-and-cream Mini, of course she did; and an order had been placed.

After a visit to the Post Office, over the road,

to withdraw the money, a deposit was paid and paperwork filled in.

Dicky also used the opportunity to make an appointment at the garage for the Austin to have its Roadworthiness Test, before he and Sophie had lunch at a little cafeteria just down the road to celebrate.

'I do hope Gerald won't mind,' Sophie said, as their plates of egg and chips arrived. 'But you have to admit it really was gorgeous.'

'Gerald did say you could do it, Sophie,' smiled Dicky. 'And he will be delighted to see how excited you are about it, I'm sure.'

There was no doubt that the stylish Mini really did look good, and Dicky could imagine that it would soon elevate Sophie and Gerald in the envious eyes of their neighbours. The car would certainly stand out, he thought.

'I hope you won't mind parking Petal on the road when it arrives,' Sophie was saying now. 'I'd like to keep the Mini on the drive to be out of harm's way.'

'Why don't you put it in the garage?' Dicky asked, taking a sip of his tea.

'That would be ideal, but unfortunately it is pretty much full of all the furniture and whatnot from Gerald's mother's place. We really must get round to sorting it out so the Mini is undercover in the winter, but Gerald seems unwilling to get on with it.'

'Too many memories perhaps?' asked Dicky. 'Of course the arrival of the Mini could be just the incentive he needs to get on with it, and I could offer to help with that.'

'Oh, would you, Dicky. I really would appreciate it.'

'Certainly,' said Dicky. 'It is the least I can do to thank you for putting me up.'

As he spoke these words it occurred to him that he had done nothing whatsoever about finding somewhere permanent to live, and now that he had a job, assuming his review of the film tonight was acceptable and they confirmed his appointment, he had no excuse not to get on with it.

'What is the furniture in there like?'

'Not too bad, a bit old-fashioned perhaps. Why do you ask?'

'I wonder, if I can find an unfurnished flat or something, if Gerald might consider selling me some of it?'

As they left the cafeteria, Dicky called briefly into the newsagents next door. On the basis that it might be wise to study the 'house style' of the publication he would be writing for, he bought a copy of 'Theatre and Cinema News, incorporating 'Box Office' to study, before he drove to Croydon to see the film.

He noticed that the shop also sold map books, and he purchased a copy of the current A-Z Street Atlas of London. The more he thought about it, the more he came to the conclusion that it would be sensible to find a place to live in London itself, if he could, and he decided to start his search as soon as he had delivered his 'copy' to the offices of his employer in the morning.

-oOo-

The Odeon, at 108, North Road, Croydon, was one of the smaller cinemas in the town and situated next to the Whitgift Centre, just off the newly constructed Croydon Underpass.

The problem Dicky encountered was how to get off the underpass and onto the road above it where the cinema was located, and he had to turn round and try again when he emerged from the deep excavation, having missed his turning.

He negotiated his way through the tangle of streets and found somewhere to park a short walk away from the cinema, arriving just in time for the film to start. He took a seat in the stalls with his notebook on his knee and noticed, as the lights started to go down, that the cinema was half empty.

'A Sweeter Taste', according to the programme and the posters in the foyer, had been a great success on the London stage in 1958, and the first surprise was that it was written by a nineteen-year-old as her first play. Now adapted into a film, to reach a broader audience, the modern drama would surprise as well as entertain, the notes declared.

Dicky was struggling to find the storyline 'entertaining'. It was set in the least salubrious part of a desolate Northern town, and mostly in what appeared to be slums. This was one of those new 'kitchen sink' dramas and the plot was designed to shock, and possibly, for those of a delicate disposition, disgust.

The earthy story revolved around a teenage girl who had an affair with a black soldier and became pregnant, and her dysfunctional relationship with her mother, whose loose morals drag the meandering story further into the gutter. The awkward plot had tried to confront issues of class, race, gender, and sex, but for Dicky it lacked cohesion, and as shock after bed-hopping shock emerged, he noticed several people walking out of the cinema, before the film had finished.

Back in the car, Dicky considered what to write. There was a dilemma to be addressed. He had noticed that several of the reviews in 'Theatre and Cinema News' were accompanied by advertisements for the plays or films in question, so the publication must derive income from advertisers wishing to promote their shows. If a reviewer damned the production, the promoters would not want to advertise, so the publication would lose money.

This was borne out by the fact that the only play, in the edition Dicky had purchased, which received a poor review was not accompanied by an advertisement.

Did his employers expect him to praise the film he had just seen to sell advertising, or was he free to write what he really thought of the tawdry and lacklustre film?

Setting his notebook on the passenger seat, Dicky resolved to think about it as he drove back to Pinner.

-oOo-

The Pigalle Club in Piccadilly was going through something of a transformation, Herbert, or Herb, Walters said.

In April the usually sedate supper club had played host to The Beatles, no less, and the management seemed determined to move it more towards becoming a popular music venue.

Dame Amelia was pleased to observe that on this evening, at least, it had returned to its more traditional style, with a pleasant jazz band who kept the volume at an acceptable level.

'We used to come here to shake a shoe regularly, Amelia. Do you remember?'

Dame Amelia did remember those evenings, although when Herb stepped on her toes on the little dance floor, the memory was not so pleasant.

They were shown to the table Herb had booked, not too near the band, and offered menus to study until their drinks arrived.

'Of course I remember everything about those evenings, Herb. How could I forget,' purred Dame Amelia. 'Now, have you had time to look at those two plays I sent you?'

She knew, of course, that Herb still had feelings for her, and he had made a bit of a pest of himself before she got married, and even proposed again a couple of months after her husband died. She hoped she had not hurt his feelings by saying it was too soon, but it was. And now that some time had passed she was perhaps being cruel by suggesting that they meet again.

If only Herb could find some nice homely girl to marry who could cook his meals and keep his house presentable. That was what he needed most in a wife, she thought.

'Yes. Ah, there is sole on the menu tonight. That was always your favourite, wasn't it. I remember hoping they would have it for you every time we met …'

'So what did you think of them?'

'And do you remember that night they ran out of champagne and that funny little waiter was sent to buy some from the restaurant next door …'

'I had forgotten that particular incident, Herb ... Now, about these plays ...'

'And after all that, you said we had better not send it back, although it wasn't cold, after all the trouble they had been to. I thought that was typical of your kind soul, Amelia. I wish that, back then ...'

'Yes, well. About those plays,' said Dame Amelia, bringing the meeting to order.

-oOo-

As Dame Amelia ordered her sole, Harry snoozed in the Bentley.

He had managed to find a parking space in an alley behind some shops a couple of streets away from the noise and bustle of Piccadilly, and covering his knees with a tartan motoring blanket, having drained the soup Mrs Childs had prepared for him in a Thermos flask, his eyes closed in sleep.

Harry knew that he must be outside the Pigalle Club at one o'clock sharp to take his employer home, and he had a secret weapon in the form of his Jaeger Memovox wristwatch, which was fitted with an alarm, to ensure he was not late. The wristwatch had belonged to Dame Amelia's last husband, and was a pre-production model. It had been given to Harry on the first anniversary of his employment with the Dame, who stressed that now he had no excuse whatsoever to be late, and there would be trouble if he was.

Harry knew it was special and probably valuable, but he did not know that its creators had given it to the late Mr Barron to thank him for putting money into their company. It was an investment that had paid off consistently and handsomely; and annually added a little more to the already substantial amounts in the vaults of Dame Amelia's bank.

-oOo-

Chapter 14

New beginnings

Dicky parked the Austin in the very same spot on Red Lion Square he had used when last he visited the offices of Sigsmund Publications.

There was no sign of Traffic Wardens this time, although he genuinely was making a delivery, rather than relying on the kindness of a fellow old soldier and film fan in the form of Traffic Warden and former Sergeant, Ernest Bacon. He intended to drop in the envelope he had prepared and drive away promptly as soon as it was done.

After careful thought, he had decided to write two separate reviews of the film he had seen the night before, along with a covering letter, and had finished typing them up at about the same time that Harry collected Dame Amelia and drove her away from Piccadilly.

The covering letter explained, he hoped, that the two reviews served different purposes and he set out his reasons for doing it.

Having decided that it was important to retain some integrity and tell the truth, the first review told it as he really saw it, but the second used gentler language and offered subtle suggestions to the reader. In this way he pointed out that he or she might find this or that aspect of the plot a little troubling, but that the author had intended them to form part of a larger picture. He made the point that, writing at just nineteen years old, a budding playwright may not have developed the ability to hint and suggest, when describing an unsavoury situation, and perhaps that was why the action was laid bare and unvarnished before the audience.

It had taken Dicky some head-scratching to come up with that idea, but he was quite pleased with the outcome and was feeling confident when he dropped his envelope into the office.

-o0o-

On the way there, Dicky had called at the offices of two large and one small estate agents, and enquired about the possibility of renting a flat near theatreland.

He had come away from that exercise shocked and disillusioned. The prices even the most modest accommodation commanded were eye-watering, and he realised he would have to think again.

It was fortunate, therefore, that he met Sergeant Ernest Bacon, the Traffic Warden, as he left the offices of Sigsmund Publications, and he was able to tell the honest fellow his troubles.

Having congratulated him on securing his new job, Sergeant Bacon listened intently while Dicky told him all about the frightful 'kitchen sink' drama he had been forced to watch the previous evening, and offered his sympathy.

'Well,' he said, 'Mrs Bacon wouldn't have liked that, and no mistake. So, if you think about it, it is a good job there are fellows like you reviewing these things. Based on the information you provide we can keep our money in our pockets to spend on something a bit more to our taste.'

Dicky saw the logic of that, although he did not explain the subtle commercial aspect of writing reviews linked to advertising revenue, which he thought he had detected in 'Theatre and Cinema News, incorporating 'Box Office'.

Dicky did, however, explain about the visits to the letting agents he had made and his disappointment at how much flats, in the area he hoped to move to, cost.

'I know what you mean,' sympathised Ernest. 'Mrs Bacon works up near there cleaning a couple of days a week, and does a couple of those flats the actors and whatnot use. They are always moaning about the costs, although most of them share, of course.'

'Share?' said Dicky.

'Yes, flat share. You know the sort of thing, where you get a bedroom of your own, but the use of the lounge and kitchen and so on is shared.'

'Yes, of course,' said Dicky. 'Do you know a flat-share had not occurred to me. It might be the answer.'

'Well, here's a funny thing … Mrs B 'does' for a nice young fellow who has a small part in 'My Fair Lady' on Drury Lane, and he lives in a flat what belongs to his dad.'

'Lucky devil,' said Dicky.

'Well, not so much. Mrs B says he only has a very small part in the show and don't earn a lot, so he has been letting off his spare bedroom to cover his costs. But the thing is the fella he has been sharing with has gone and joined the Royal Shakespeare Company in Stratford, so is going to move out. Mrs B said the young fella was quite worried about whether he would be able to afford to keep paying her to 'do' unless he found someone to take the spare room.'

'Gosh!' said Dicky, 'Where did you say this flat was?'

'It's round the corner from all the theatres, in Dean Street, I think it is. It's an odd sort of arrangement though, the lower floors is all offices with just a couple of flats up top. Mrs B has to use the lift that goes through the offices to get there.'

'Look, this is a bit of a cheek,' said Dicky, 'but do you think Mrs Bacon would be prepared to put me in touch with this gentleman? The location sounds ideal and I really wouldn't mind sharing if it keeps the costs under control.'

'I can do better than that, young fella-me-lad. Mrs B is due to 'do' that place this very afternoon, and if you will pay for the call, I will telephone her, and ask her to ask him. How's that?'

'Sergeant Bacon, that is wonderful! Thank you very much.'

-oOo-

Carefully getting out of the boat, in her over-large wellies, Camilla stood and looked at the castle towering above her.

From this side you could see that a considerable amount of the original structure had fallen down over the years, and the weeds barely concealed vast heaps of lichen- covered stones which had once been part of the structure, left where they had fallen.

Facing them was a steepish path, with steps cut roughly into the ground, leading to an arched doorway with a tall and substantial looking wooden door.

'Nearly there,' said Hamish, jangling a substantial bunch of keys. 'I've no' put the heating on, but if you hang on I'll start yon generator so we can use the lights.'

With that he loped off towards a semi-derelict stone building which contained the machinery, and which was soon belching out thick black smoke as the engine started.

'I'll need to get the mechanic tay give that the once-over before we get any guests,' spluttered Hamish as he rejoined them and indicated that they should proceed up the path to the doorway.

As they climbed up now, Camilla was aware of a low whistling wind which seemed to be singing a melancholy song around the castle walls.

'Hear that, Milly? That's the ghosts of a hundred dead who once stormed the castle and were slaughtered in boiling oil poured from the ramparts up there,' Annie was pointing to a platform high above them.'

'Ah, get on wi' you!' chuckled Hamish. 'Yon platform was left by the roofing contractors who put the new roof on last year! You have to make allowances, she is a Campbell, and it was once them that tried to storm the ruddy castle. Perhaps my ancestors would have been wiser just to give them the blasted place. It would have saved a lot of expense for my generation!'

-oOo-

Now safely tucked up in his bed, Harry's alarm made no impression on him at all, and after his long night waiting uncomfortably in the car, he slept on until after ten o'clock.

Dame Amelia, on the other hand, was up and doing a little before eight o'clock, and was to be found writing letters in the library when Simpkin arrived with her morning coffee.

'Good morning, ma'am,' he intoned, in the special subdued voice he reserved for days when those he was addressing might conceivably have a headache. 'I trust you had a pleasant evening?'

'Capital, thank you Simpkin,' smiled the Dame.

She was looking, Simpkin noticed, as fresh as a daisy.

'I am expecting a call from Herb … er, Sir Herbert Walters a little later. If I am walking in the garden when it comes through, please be sure to ask him to hold the line while you fetch me. I do not want to miss his call.'

'Very good, Ma'am,' said Simpkin, quietly pleased. 'Will that be all?'

-oOo-

At seven o'clock in the evening, Dicky was standing

outside the telephone box at the end of the road, counting his money. He was about to call Sgt. Ernest Bacon and find out if Mrs Bacon had spoken to the young man about sharing his flat, and if so, what the outcome was.

Before they parted, they had agreed that Dicky would make this call to coincide with Mrs Bacon's return from work and Sgt. Bacon coming off duty and returning home for his supper.

Glancing at his watch and registering that he had two more minutes to wait before putting in the call, Dicky thought about what an inconvenience it was not to have a telephone in the house.

He knew that many regarded telephones as an expensive luxury, and realised that for most people they had a point, but in this modern era it was becoming increasingly difficult to get along without one.

He hoped that the flat he was going to discuss with Sgt. Bacon had a telephone, and more than that, he hoped the young man in residence would consider sharing with him.

He had discussed the idea at length with Sophie and Gerald, and when he revealed the staggering rent he had discovered was being charged for a self-contained flat, they conceded that a 'flat-share' might be his best option.

Gerald was kind enough to point out that there was

no hurry for him to move out of their house, and Sophie added that it would be better to take his time and find the right thing. But Dicky felt that he had had a series of really lucky breaks lately, which certainly went against the normal run of things, and he was anxious to make the best of his winning streak while it lasted.

He took a deep breath now, and stepped into the telephone box.

-oOo-

Chapter 15

Two tests

The second call Dicky made followed close on the heels of the first.

Mrs Bacon had been given permission to pass on the number of the nice young man who was looking to share his flat, and Dicky wasted no time in seizing the opportunity to make contact.

'Hullo? Hullo? Is that David?' Dicky asked as the call connected and his money dropped into the box. 'This is Richard Bourne, Mrs Bacon may have mentioned...'

'Oh, hello there. Mrs B said your name was Dicky, but no matter. Thank you for calling.'

'Yes. They know me as Dicky, most people do. I wondered if...'

'Yes, of course, come round for a look any time after about noon tomorrow if you like. I'm afraid I have to dash off to work now, so do you mind if we cut this short and discuss the finer details when we meet?'

'That's fine. Noon tomorrow. What is the address, please.'

'Flat B, 9-11, Richmond Buildings, London, W1. It's off Richmond Mews which is a turning off Dean Street. If you come by car there is little parking area down a ramp off the Mews. If you pick up the phone in the tin box by the gate and press button 'B', I can let you in.'

'The flat has parking? ...' asked Dicky in astonishment.

'Yes, Look I'm sorry I really do have to go now. I shall look forward to meeting you tomorrow, Richard … er, Dicky.'

-oOo-

As one leaf of the tall double door swung open to admit them, Annie sighed.

'I've not been in here since I was a wee girl,' she said. 'We used to run about all over the castle back then.'

'That we did,' added Hamish.

'Until they condemned it as a "dangerous structure" that was, and then Uncle Jock wouldn't even let us come over to the island on the boat.'

'Aye, but d'ye remember the bedtime stories he used to weave around the place?'

'And scared us half to death, you mean!' smiled Annie. 'I swear his tales of ghosts and evil beasties knocked years off my young life.'

'Anyway, come on in and see what we've done with the place!' laughed Hamish, leading the way.

-oOo-

Dicky had had trouble sleeping, and over breakfast Sophie commented that he was like a cat on a hot tin roof.

'Sorry, Sophie, I'm just excited,' smiled Dicky. 'Do you have any change for the telephone? I've almost run out and have to call the office first thing.'

'The amount of time you spend in that telephone box, Dicky! The neighbours will think we make you sleep in it!'

'Their office opens at half past nine, you see. And I want to find out what they thought of my reviews ...'

'Here you are,' said Sophie handing over some coins. 'There is about five-bob's worth there and I shall want it back.'

'Thanks, Sis,' and with that Dicky was up from the table and reaching for his jacket.

-o0o-

'I don't suppose Camilla will mind, Herb,' said Dame Amelia into the telephone. 'But she left me no forwarding number in Scotland, so I can't get hold of her. She will be back by then, of course.'

'Well, it is very kind of you to invite me, Amelia, and of course I shall be delighted to come. It is some considerable time since I went to a weekend house party, and I've never been to Holme Hall, so it will be a new experience.'

'Yes, well, as I said, it all depends on this young budding playwright. If he can't come we shall have to cancel, of course. But he seemed very smitten with Camilla.'

'So she is the bait to get him there, then.'

'Herb! What a thing to say! It doesn't really matter about Camilla being here, it is those plays we need to discuss. I'm so glad you liked them as much as I did.'

'Ah, well, I've been meaning to talk to you about that,' said Herb uncomfortably. 'There are a few issues with the text, especially in some of the dialogue, we should have to iron out before …'

'Yes, yes. Well I can leave all that sort of thing to you, Herb, of course. But I did think the character of the elegant dowager in the first play was particularly well drawn. I shall want to talk to you about her.'

-oOo-

Once again it seemed to take an age for Captain White to come to the telephone and Dicky was kept busy shovelling coins into the box while he waited. But his patience, and investment, was rewarded when, at last, Captain White came on the line.

'Most impressed. Yes, most impressed. The second review was very perceptive and nicely written. We would have published that if we were really looking to do a review of that revolting film.'

'You know the film then?'

'Well, no. But I've seen the play and thought it was ghastly. You neatly captured the essence of it in your writing and put it very well, I thought.'

'What about this issue with advertising revenue?'

'Ah, well I'd like to talk to you about that properly when you join us here in the office.'

'You mean you are prepared to confirm my appointment?'

'Certainly. Can you start at nine-fifteen next Monday?'

-oOo-

Dicky had to rush now.

The little Austin was due at the garage for its test

and he hoped it would not delay him getting to the flat for noon.

'Good luck, Petal,' said Sophie, giving the bonnet an affectionate pat. 'I'm sure there is nothing expensive wrong with her.'

'I hope not, and it is going to cost me fourteen-bob to find out.'

-oOo-

The dining hall on the lower floor was certainly large, and as Hamish turned on the flickering strip lights, it was revealed in all its grandeur.

'Baronial,' said Camilla.

'Bloody difficult to heat,' said Hamish.

'An opportunity to make a real statement, with the right furnishings and decor,' said Annie. 'What the heck is that midget-sized suit of armour doing in here?'

'Is that real?' asked Camilla.

'Ah,' said Hamish. He rather liked the diminutive modern tin imitation.

-oOo-

''Ad an 'ard life, ain't it? All them dents and scratches … Mind you, at that age I would 'ave expected more rust, and at least there is plenty of tread left on them tyres.'

The ruddy-faced mechanic at the garage had finished his inspection and was about to give his verdict on the little old Austin.

"An although there is some wear in them king-pins that you will 'ave to attend to 'fore much longer, there ain't much else wrong with it.'

'So has she, I mean it, passed?' asked Dicky.

'Yes. Come with me, chum, and we can attend to the paperwork, and that.'

Dicky let out a huge sigh of relief, and handed over his fourteen shillings without a murmur.

'If you wos interested, we could change them king-pins and do a full service at the same time. Gawd knows when it last had an oil change. The stuff in there is like treacle, an' the brake shoes ain't got that much life left in them, you know.'

'Oh, I think that will all have to wait until I have had my first couple of month's wages. Just out of interest, how much would that cost?' Dicky asked.

As he drove out of the garage, Dicky patted the dashboard of the little car.

'Well done, Petal,' he said. 'But I'm afraid we are either going to have to find somewhere considerably cheaper or you are going to have to hang on for a bit for new king-pins, or whatever they are called, and a service, old girl.'

Chapter 16

Paradise found?

Dicky drove twice round Richmond Mews until he spotted the shallow ramp he had been told led to the car parking area.

Carefully applying the handbrake on the slope, remembering what the florid mechanic had said about the brake shoes, he opened the car door and approached a metal box, hinged on one side, which opened to reveal a white telephone handset and a series of buttons.

Pressing 'button B' now, Dicky waited, and took a more detailed look at the building he was facing.

9-11, Richmond Buildings, was obviously recently built, at least in part, although it adjoined another older structure, part of which was built out over the road and connected it to a bigger office. Dicky wondered if it was one of the many bomb-damaged buildings which had been rebuilt after the war.

The higgledy-piggledy buildings in the mews all seemed to date from different periods, and had various architectural styles, and stepping back a little for a better look, Dicky could see that most were used as offices.

The building he sought to enter now was also obviously an office and for a moment he wondered if he was in the right place. But then a voice answered the telephone in his hand.

'Lo?'

'Er, David? It's Dicky.'

'Oh, right. Yes. Sorry. Push the gate and you will see the door leading to the hall. Take the lift to the fifth floor. Are you in a car?'

'Er, yes …'

'Park in one of the two spaces on the right then, and I'll see you in a minute.'

Dicky heard the metal gate give a click, and a gentle push made it open inwards, away from the street. Dicky drove through and hopped out to close the gate behind him.

Parking as directed, he noticed he was in a small semi-underground area with about five parking slots, and to the rear, grills on openings at eye level revealed a small but very well presented garden area, accessed, he assumed, from somewhere within the building.

The doorway leading to the hallway had five wide steps up and then opened up into a rather well appointed foyer area, decorated in what looked like green marble.

Ahead there was a reception desk and a glass door leading to the street, and facing him there was a lift. He pressed the call button, and as he waited, he touched the green material on the walls. It was warm to the touch, and therefore not marble but some sort of plastic, he decided.

Exiting the lift on the fifth floor he was greeted by David himself, in bedroom slippers and a dressing gown.

'Hello, Dicky. Nice to meet you,' he said. 'You will have to forgive me, I've only just woken up. You see there was a party after the show last night and ...'

'Not to worry,' said Dicky. 'I suppose, being on the stage, you are unlikely to be able to keep regular hours.'

'Quite right,' said David, ushering him into a well-appointed and spacious hall, decorated with Victorian-style cornices and dotted about with stylish mirrors and side tables. 'We theatrical types habitually fail to get up before noon. And Sebastian, my current sharer, wouldn't get up at all if it was up to him.'

'Mrs Bacon said …'

'Yes, the lucky blighter has struck the big time and is off to Stratford-upon-Avon to mess about with the works of the bard. And doesn't he go on about it! "Life is as tedious as a twice-told tale, Vexing the dull ear of a drowsy man," as King John put it.'

'So when does he leave?'

'Soon enough, but he leaves me in a somewhat difficult position. I'm just "A poor player that struts and frets his hour upon the stage, and then is heard no more" - "Macbeth" - you see. So finding someone to share with is something of a necessity.'

'So, when do you think …'

'Next Tuesday. He is paid-up until next Tuesday. "All the world's a stage, and all the men and women merely players. They have their exits and their entrances; And one man in his time plays many parts." - "As You Like It".. Come on, I'll show you round.'

Dicky obediently followed him into the spacious and rather elegantly furnished lounge and his mood changed to one of gloom. There had been no talk of money yet but he could see at a glance that he would not be able to afford to live in such a grand place.

'There is a little balcony that looks out on a bit of

garden here,' David explained.

'No Shakespearean quote about the garden, then?' smiled Dicky.

'I'm sorry, you must forgive me. That is an appalling nervous habit. Actors endlessly fling quotations at each other in an attempt to prove that they can learn their lines, and whenever one meets a stranger it is all too easy to slip into 'audition mode', where that sort of behaviour is quite acceptable. It shan't happen again.'

'This place is lovely,' said Dicky as David ushered him through the stylishly furnished dining room and on to the spacious kitchen, 'but I don't think I could afford anything like this ...'

'I thought you might say that, Dicky, old man. But you haven't seen my secret weapon yet, and the reason why you may well be able to afford such luxury, after all.'

'What do you mean?'

'How are you with a paintbrush? Ever done any wallpapering?'

'I don't understand. It all looks recently decorated.'

'It is, but you have not yet seen Sebastian's room.' David moved across the hall and rested his hand on the door handle. 'Thinking Sebastian would be with me forever, just before I left for a short holiday, I foolishly agreed that Sebastian could decorate his room however he liked, and this, I'm afraid, is the result.'

With a flourish, and a theatrical wave of his arm, David threw open the door to Sebastian's domain. What was revealed caused Dicky to gasp.

The ceiling, up to the decorative cornices, had been painted black, as were two of the walls. A third wall was a lurid green, relieved, if that is the right word, by giant, multi-coloured cartoonish flowers, and the forth wall, where the door was opened, was purple with yellow speckles which looked as though a paintbrush had been used to flick them onto the surface.

'Sebastian, until he got a shop … I'm sorry, "Theatre Speak", I should have said until he was taken on by a theatre company to act in a Shakespearian play, had visions of throwing up acting and becoming an artist. I learned later, from his mother, that he did something similar at his family home.'

Dicky was still reeling from the shock and struggling for something to say.

'Er … how did you feel about this when you got back from your trip?'

'Well, I was horrified, of course, but at that time I was resting … that is to say I was between acting roles, so with bills to pay, I was in no position to throw him out, much as I might have liked to. I complained to his mother, but beyond that I had no other sanctions to impose on him.'

'But surely he will put it right before he leaves, won't he?'

'Ah, there you take me into deep waters. You see Sebastian is in love. It is a fairly recent thing and related to his move to Shakespearian Stratford. He has not been back here for some weeks, much to Mrs B's delight, and now has cut off all contact.
When I said he is moving out on Tuesday, I'm afraid I stretched the truth a little. Tuesday is when his rent is paid-up to. I have it on good authority, from his mother, that he is not coming back and is not going to pay any further instalments. I may, she informed me, retain the paltry deposit he gave me when he moved in, but that will only just pay for the paint, not the labour to correct this horror.'

Dicky had been trying to look past the decor as David spoke and realised that the room was spacious, with a large picture window, a big built-in wardrobe and a view over the little garden below he had seen on the way in. Before this decorative disaster was inflicted on it, it must have been a very pleasant room.

'And the other thing,' David was saying, 'is that bed, that double bed you see, is broken. Somehow or other, and one does not like to enquire too deeply, Sebastian has snapped the frame in the middle, and the mattress was damaged at the same time. So you see, Dicky, old man, that your concerns about being able to afford to live in such a place as this could be unfounded, so long as you are prepared to stump up for a new bed and return the decor to something more appropriate for the home of an English gentleman.

Dicky swallowed hard.

'So, if I undertook to do the work and got a new bed, what sort of rent would you charge?' he asked.

'Before we touch on the fiscal aspect, I have just one more condition to impose.'

'Oh?' said Dicky.

'I understand from the lovely and ever reliable Mrs B, that you do reviews for 'The Critical Review'.'

'Well, not yet, but I will be after next Monday, when I start work there,' admitted Dicky.

'Well, so long as you promise never to slate any performance of mine in that august magazine, and do the work as discussed to a good and workmanlike standard, I think we can move forward.'

Dicky smiled at that and asked David to name a figure. It was affordable, just, and he immediately agreed and held out his hand to shake.

'You don't realise it, but you may have actually just saved my life. "Your name from hence immortal life shall have," - Sonnet 81 … Oh, I'm so sorry. Please forgive me. But you don't know how relieved I am to have some financial certainty at last!'

'Are things that bad? I know Mrs B was worried that you would not be able to retain her services ...'

'It is not that so much. There is a bigger picture, as they say. You see my father owns this building. His company had its offices here before he retired, or rather semi-retired from business, and now he rents it all off. He used to use the other one of the two flats up here as his base when in town, but now it is rented out, and this flat should be too. But although he constantly reminds me how generous he is being, he lets me have this place at an advantageous price so long as I see to it that the bills are paid.'

'Well, that sounds ...'

'Ah, but the thing is, Dicky, old man, a place such as this, in the desirable setting that it enjoys, comes with eye-watering service charges, rates and what-have-you, and being in a somewhat precarious profession, dangerously close to the bottom of the pile, paying all that is a constant worry to a gentle soul like me.'

'Well, I have to say our arrangement suits me down to the ground, and so long as you accept that I shall have to do the decorating myself, rather than pay a professional, which I doubt if I could afford, then I'm very happy.'

'Wonderful. Just wonderful. I can see that we shall be very happy together!' said David. 'Oh, and by the way, did I tell you that one of the parking spaces downstairs comes with the flat, and as buying any form of motorised transport is but a pipe-dream for me, you are welcome to use it.'

Suddenly unable to speak, Dicky shook David's hand again.

-oOo-

'Well, I could help you,' said Sophie. 'I decorated the lounge, the bedroom you use and the kitchen here, you know.'

'Did you, Sis? I had no idea.'

'And there is a double bed frame in the garage if it helps, although there is no mattress.'

'But won't Gerald want to sell all that stuff?'

'If you give us a hand to get rid of it, I'm sure we could call the bed frame your reward.'

'Have you decided what to do with it?'

'Well, having now confirmed that we have failed to flog any of it to you, we have a second plan. We shall put it into an auction and if it makes any money that will be a bonus. At least when it is gone we can get the Mini in the garage.'

'That reminds me, I've got to go to the insurance broker's office in the High Street tomorrow to fix up insurance for the Austin. Do you want to come and sort yours out for the new Mini?'

'An excellent idea, Dicky, and afterwards you can take me for a cuppa at that new foreign delicatessen place just along from there. I hear it is very interesting.'

-oOo-

Chapter 17

A surprise, or two

Hamish looked at Camilla in astonishment.

'What, musicians? Well, I would nay thought of that in a month of Sundays. I'm not sure, mind. Tents, you say?'

'Isn't it obvious, Hamish,' interjected Annie. 'People will need to travel so will want to stay, and that means we could hold the event over two days and offer camping facilities.'

'Let them pitch wee tents on yon grass?'

'Yes, but you had better mow it first, or it will be too wet,' said Camilla.

'And where will we get these musicians?'

'You leave that to me, Hamish, my boy,' said Annie, pulling herself up to her full height, such as it was.

'I propose to talk to Heather McCormack, you know, from Heather and the Heartaches. We go way back, and I bet she knows loads of people in the showbiz.'

'But it is a wee bit remote here for something like that, don't ye think? Will people come?'

'While you have still got the railway, before they close it down, it is quite easy to get here, actually,' said Camilla. 'And the main roads are not bad at all, if you don't get lost.'

'Don't rub it in, Milly. I know where I went wrong. We would have been fine if I'd kept on the 'A' road.'

'Mebbe the bus company could run folk from the station,' said Hamish, warming to the idea.'

'And you could make a car park in the stoney field on the other side of the drive,' added Annie.

'That one?' said Hamish pointing. 'Nothing much grows there. Too little soil over the bed rock.'

'Precisely. The ideal place to park cars.'

'I have thought of one problem,' said Camilla. 'Toilets. I don't suppose you would want that many people traipsing in and out of the house …'

'How many people d'ye think will come then?'

'Oh, probably only a hundred or so … in the first year,' said Annie airily. 'But if it takes off and gets a bit of a reputation, we could repeat it. Then loads more would come, each year perhaps.'

'A hundred people tramping through ma hoos! I don't think so!'

'Well, we must think of another solution. What happened to all the muck when you used to keep cows up at the byre on the top there.'

Annie was pointing to an ancient building, now with a sagging roof, which was once a cow shed and milking parlour, installed in the days when dairy farming was profitable and a substantial herd roamed these fields.

'Down the bank is the old midden,' said Hamish. 'The septic tank for the main hoos is over there too.'

'Well, there you are!' exclaimed Camilla. 'Put some loos in there!'

'Och! And wha' d'ya think that'll cost, young lady?'

'You will have to be prepared to speculate to accumulate, as the saying goes, Hamish,' announced Annie. 'You will have to do it with the decor in the castle, so this is just another bit of that jigsaw.'

'And it won't be just for one thing,' said Camilla. 'What about setting up a camping ground here for people, you know, hikers and that sort of thing, to camp and have a holiday?'

'A camp site, ye mean?' Hamish scratched his chin. 'It's a thought.'

-oOo-

Just as Dicky was coming down the stairs for breakfast, the letter box flap was lifted and three letters fluttered onto the mat. He absentmindedly picked them up and carried them through to the dining room where Sophie was laying out the breakfast things.

'Good morning, Sis,' he said. 'You've got some post.'

Sophie took the envelopes and glanced at them.

'Bills' she said, laying aside two brown envelopes. 'But what's this?'

The envelope she now held was cream in colour and obviously made from expensive paper.

'Oh, it's for you,' Sophie sounded disappointed. 'Is it a love letter?'

The handwriting on the envelope was neat and precise and obviously written with a fountain pen. Dicky did not recognise it, but his heart skipped a beat when he noticed the post mark. The letter had been posted at Woodlesham, in Surrey.

Dicky sat down at the table.

'Well? Aren't you going to open it?' asked Sophie, intrigued.

-oOo-

'So there you have it, Uncle Jock,' said Annie. 'What do you think?'

Jock wasn't really Annie's uncle, of course, but was adopted as such as she and Hamish grew up. She had always addressed him as Uncle and continued to do so now.

'Weel, it'll take some thinking aboot,' said the ancient little man, smiling. 'But on the whole it seems a great plan.'

'You like it! Oh, Uncle Jock, I hoped you would, but I thought you might say no!'

'Och, Annie. The young must have fun. In ma' time such a thing was inconceivable, of course, but why not? Ah think it is a terrific idea.'

'Well, that's a surprise,' said Hamish. 'But d'ye think we can afford it?'

-oOo-

With the arrival of the letter, of course, Dicky had the telephone number of Holme Hall, which was printed under the address on the elegant notepaper.

The invitation was hand-written and there was no mention of whether Camilla would be there, but it struck Dicky that it was certainly a possibility.

In her note Dame Barron-Zukor had explained that she had read both his plays and thanked him for sending them. She mentioned that she particularly liked one of them, which she wanted to talk to him about. She also said that if he could join them for the weekend on the dates she set out, they would be having a small house party and there may be one or two people he might like to meet who would be interested in his writing.

She closed by asking him to telephone and accept the invitation at his earliest convenience and confirm whether he would like her to send her car to collect him.

Dicky had to read the letter twice more before he was certain it was real, and could tell his sister about it.

The radio, habitually on for the news while they had breakfast, was burbling about US President John F. Kennedy's visit to West Berlin. He stood in front of the Berlin Wall and gave a speech to more than ten thousand West Berliners, the newsreader announced. And a tape-recording of him saying 'Ich bin ein Berliner', was played followed by an explanation saying his words meant 'I am a Berliner', and that showed that America stood side-by-side with the people of West Berlin.

Sophie listened, enraptured, but although Dicky had actually stood in front of this manifestation of the 'Iron Curtain', or the 'Wall of Shame', as some called it, he was too engrossed in Dame Amelia's letter to take much notice.

'At least that wall stopped the problem with all those economic migrants trying to get to the West,' she said under her breath.

They had arranged to be at the flat at noon, to give David time to get up, and now the boot of the little Austin was full of paint cans, brushes and the paraphernalia required for decorating the bedroom.

As the time approached for them to leave the house, Dicky, dressed in his oldest clothes, was anxious to be off. But Sophie was fussing with stacks of newspapers which she insisted they must spread over the floor to prevent spillages and accidents with the paint.

'We don't want to ruin the carpet, do we? You will have quite enough expense, from what you say about this place, without having to buy a new carpet.'

'Fair enough,' said Dicky. 'You are right, of course, Sis. I had no idea that paint and all that equipment was so expensive. No wonder David didn't want to do the job himself.'

-oOo-

Earlier, Dicky had dialled the number printed on the letter from the telephone box at the end of the road, and been told by the butler that Dame Amelia was out.

He left a message confirming that he would be delighted to accept his invitation, and after a moment of hesitation, asked the butler if he would be expected to dress for dinner.

'Dame Amelia lived for many years in the United States of America, where it was acceptable to dispense with the formality of correct evening dress, sir,' said the butler stiffly. 'Guests will be expected to wear lounge suits only, I fancy.'

Dicky exhaled in relief. The cost of hiring formal wear was something he could do without.

'Will you be requiring the car, sir?' asked the butler.

'Er, no thank you. I can drive myself down.'

'Very good, sir. There may be an opportunity to use the tennis lawn, or to swim in the pool, if you would like to bring appropriate dress for those activities, sir.'

Tennis, and swimming? Dicky was impressed.

'Thank you,' he said. 'I'll bear that in mind.'

-oOo-

Chapter 18

Two days later

Annie had made quite sure of the route this time, and after the sole overnight stop they planned was behind them, she was more confident as their journey back to London got underway again in Camilla's MG Midget.

'So the plan is to go straight to my flat, and you go off and talk to these fabric suppliers and what-have-you with Hamish first thing in the morning.'

'Yes. Are you sure you don't mind us borrowing your car and trailing round to see all these cloth mill companies and furniture places, Milly? I hope it won't take too long.'

Camilla had spent the last few days holding the end of a tape measure and watching Annie produce rather lovely sketches of how she saw the furniture and decoration being arranged inside the castle. She had not appreciated quite how accomplished an artist Annie was, and thought some of her sketches were worthy of being framed.

'Having been involved in the process so far, I'm beginning to find it fascinating and I'm anxious to see how it all comes out. And anyway, it will be much easier to run round to these places in the car than fiddle about with buses or taxis.'

'And it's kind of you to let us stay at your place, Milly, and I'm very glad to be able to use the car. I really must try to save up enough money to get a car of my own, and to take driving lessons, of course, so I can be a wee bit more independent.'

'And Hamish will be arriving this afternoon. I've given him the spare keys of the flat and told him to make himself at home, if he arrives before we do,' said Camilla. 'Do you think he will be able to find it, and will he be all right on his own until we get back?'

'I've told him to get a taxi from the station, so he does nay get lost. He said he could walk to save some money, but I told him he might be walking around in circles for hours trying to find it, and not to be such a skinflint.'

'I don't think he really is a meanie, I think it is just an act.' Camilla stated.

'You haven't known him as long as I have, Milly. He has always had what you might call "one-way pockets", money can go in but it does nay come out!'

'You obviously like him though ...'

'It's funny. For years our relationship has been a brother and sister sort of thing. We grew up together after all. But since he got back from his National Service ... I don't know, what it is, but he doesn't seem so much like a wee boy anymore.'

'I've seen the way you look at him, Annie. Go on, admit it ...'

'Oh, stop!' giggled Annie. 'I've been having quite a hard time examining how I feel about him on this visit, if I'm honest. We think we know everything there is to know about someone, and then ... and then ...'

-oOo-

Sophie had been marvellous, and had literally and metaphorically rolled her sleeves up to help Dicky with the decorating.

For the last couple of days she had accompanied him as he worked at the flat and together they did their best to cover up the ghastly paint daubed on the walls and ceiling, left by the departing Sebastian.

After a somewhat unsuccessful attempt to cover the black paint with two coats of white, Dicky agreed with David that the best plan was to purchase some 'Anaglypta' textured wallpaper and line the ceiling and the walls with it, and then paint over it.

This was an extra expense for Dicky, of course, but after two days of trying and failing to cover up the black paint particularly, he was glad to find a solution that would bring the job to an end, so that he could take up occupancy of the room.

For a wallpapering table, they used the broken bed frame and the sheet of hardboard Sebastian had placed on it, to enable him to continue use it without ending up on the floor, or impaling himself on protruding springs.

Work was now proceeding at pace, and progress could be seen. Sophie had proved particularly adept at papering the ceiling, having done it once before with her husband, when they moved into their house.

Paying little heed to the wallpaper glue which inevitably got on her clothes and in her hair, until she started wearing a shower cap, Sophie wrestled with the wallpaper with determination, and finally, at last, the thick paper was up.

Now, as they drove to the flat again, they both hoped the wallpaper would still be where they left it the previous night, so that painting could begin.

-oOo-

As Dicky and Sophie stopped the little Austin on the ramp leading to the parking area, and Dicky got out to use the telephone handset in the metal box by the gate, and press 'button B' to alert David to their arrival, a taxi drew up beside them.

Dicky, engrossed in dealing with the mechanics of the gate, as David remotely released the lock, took no notice, until he was arrested by a sharp cry and a voice immediately behind him.

'Ma God! Dicky, it *is* you! Wah, in the name of all that is holy are y'doing here?'

Dicky spun round and lost his grip on the metal gate as Hamish stood before him.

As the gate clanged against the wall it was Dicky's turn to let out an exclamation.

'Hamish! What on earth? ...'

-oOo-

Chapter 19

Reunions

'Yes, I'm staying here tonight wi' a friend of a friend, so I can visit some contacts of Annie, the wee gurrl who is doing the interior design stuff fer the castle.'

'Well, I never. What a coincidence meeting you!' said Dicky, clasping his hand. 'This is my sister, Sophie. We are doing some decorating to a flat here ...'

'Is thus how y'are making a living, Dicky? Painting and decorating?'

'No, you don't understand, Hamish. Let me explain.'

A little later, while Sophie started putting the first coat of paint on the paper, which was mercifully still stuck in place, Dicky and Hamish made tea in the kitchen and caught up.

As they talked, David bustled about around them, preparing his late breakfast.

'Won't your host be expecting you?' Dicky asked.

'Not yet, there is nobody in their flat at present. I'm tay wait here for them.'

'New people moved in there recently,' observed David, buttering toast.

-oOo-

'I believe she will be back at her apartment this evening, Simpkin, but I shall be out.
Could you telephone her and tell her to meet me for lunch at "Le Caprice", tomorrow at one o'clock and then call the restaurant and make a booking for the two of us, at my usual table.?.'

'Certainly, ma'am,' said Simpkin, the butler.
'And then would you be so good as to inform Jarvis that he is to drive me to "Le Caprice" in St James', to arrive at ten minutes past one tomorrow.'

'Ten past one, ma'am?'

'Yes, that is the average amount of time my daughter is late for her engagements, so we should arrive together.'

'Very good, ma'am.'

'Oh, and Simpkin, you are to impress on my daughter that I wish to discuss an important matter with her and I expect her to keep this luncheon date. Please make it clear that I will not accept any excuses.'

-oOo-

'So tomorrow afternoon,' stated Annie, as the MG crawled along in heavy traffic on the outskirts of town, 'I'm to phone up Heather McCormack and agree where we can meet. It was lucky that I got hold of her when I did, she is only in London for a week and then off to some ghastly Working Man's Club in Worksop or somewhere equally grim next week.'

'Are you sure about this?' asked Camilla. 'Do you really think the idea of an open air concert could take off? It was only an idle thought that came to me when I first glimpsed the castle.'

'It could be really terrific, Milly. But it will only come together if we work at it.' Annie smiled as the traffic began to untangle itself. 'Thank goodness we are moving again! Did you see that car with its bonnet up and steam pouring out? I was worried that would happen to us if we didn't get going soon.'

'Yes. Hamish will probably be there by now and will be wondering what has happened to us.'

'Och! Don't worry about him, Milly. He will probably have found some nice cozy pub to wait in.'

-oOo-

'Yes, 'My Fair Lady' has been at the Theatre Royal, Drury Lane, since 1958, and five years is a remarkable run for any show.'

David was responding to Hamish's polite enquiries as to what he did for work.

'There have been several changes to the cast since then, and I'm a bit fearful because the management have scheduled a review of the finances in October,' David pulled a face. 'The bean counters are always hot on our heels and I have to confess we have not always enjoyed full houses recently. "Of all base passions, fear is most accursed,"
- Henry VI, Part 1, I think'

'What part do you play?' asked Hamish.

'Oh, only a minor role. I'm officially the 'second flunky' on the programme, although I also understudy one of the bigger parts, in case of illness, or whatever.'

Dicky, who was now painting alongside his sister in the bedroom with the door ajar, called out, 'I'm sure they will always need a flunky, David!'

'Nice of you to say so, Dicky, "Thou art wise as thou art beautiful" - A Midsummer Night's Dream,' laughed David. 'And I hope you are right!'

'Och!' said Hamish. 'Is that the lift? I'd better see if Annie and her friend are back ... So, are we on fer a beer tonight if I'm allowed oot, Dicky?'

'I can't see why not. I have to drop Sophie home first, at tea time of course, but if I come back up, I can get on with a bit more painting and try to break the back of this job tonight, then we could find a pub for a drink.'

'I'd recommend 'The York Minster' at the end of Dean Street,' said David, 'Best pub round here, I'd say.'

-oOo-

As a plan, that worked out well.

As Dicky went down to the car park with Sophie he noticed that there was a blue MG Midget in one of the other parking places, and it reminded him of Camilla again. He remembered seeing a blue MG coming out of the drive of Holme Hall. Although it was only a glimpse, that was the last time he had seen Camilla, and although this car was much dirtier than the one she had been driving then, it served to remind him how much he was hoping Camilla would be there when he went down to Surrey for the weekend with her mother.

For the first time he began to feel nervous about the prospect of this weekend in the country, and he found his mouth was very dry. He was looking forward to his beer with Hamish later, when he would tell his old friend how love at first sight had come to him, and all about finding Camilla.

-oOo-

It was wonderful to catch up with Hamish again over a beer, and to hear all about his efforts to make some money out of the old castle.

Hamish told him at length all about his old friend and neighbour, Annie, and how they grew up together. Dicky noticed the old familiar signs as he enthused about her.

'So, you and this Annie then ...' Dicky said.

'I don't mind admitting it. I've no seen her for a while, y'ken, but ... well, she has certainly grown up since we were kids together.'

Only a passing reference was made to the owner of the flat he was staying in, although he did say that the 'nice wee gurrl' who lived there had come up with a novel idea for an open-air music event at the castle, which was worrying him. He was explaining the problems he saw with that, when, all too soon, it was time for Dicky to say good night and drive back to Pinner.

-oOo-

As Dicky and Hamish were saying their farewells down the road from the flat, in The York Minster pub, Harry Jarvis, the chauffeur, was talking to a doorman of his acquaintance.

He worked at Quaglino's in Bury Street, just

round the corner from the Fortnum and Mason department store where, in a little service road, Harry had parked the Bentley.

Dame Amelia was meeting a group of friends at Quaglino's, and Harry suspected he was in for another late night.

'You should have been here yesterday evening, Harry. Right old caper it was,' the doorman was saying.
'That John Profumo bloke, you know, the War Minister, and his wife made an embarrassing exhibition of themselves by dancing, all lovey-dovey like, and there was photographers here too.
'And would you credit that, after it was all over the bloomin' newspapers last weekend that he had been sleeping with that Christine Keeler … You know the rumour, of course; that she has been at it with him as well as with a Soviet spy. Bloke called Ivanov, if I've got the name right.
'Now here he was, as bold as brass, with his wife, smooching in public and trying to make out everything was normal.
'Being a dirty cow and sleeping around is one thing, but they reckon that Christine Keeler was slipping the Soviet bloke secrets during what you might call their pillow talk. There is no limit to what these political types will get up to, it seems.'

'Well, he won't be getting my vote,' said Harry.

'You see it all here at Quaglino's,' said the doorman.

'What a place! I dunno how you stand it,' said Harry, shaking his head.

-oOo-

Chapter 20

New horizons

Clearing out the garage took on an unexpected urgency when Sophie announced that the new Mini was due to arrive. But, thanks to the efforts of three men and a lorry from the auction house, it was not nearly as onerous as it might have been.

Now left with just the metal bed frame to remove, Dicky was pleased to see that it simply bolted together, and borrowing the tools from Gerald, he soon had it apart in manageable sections and stowed in the little Austin ready for the drive to London.

There was no room in the car for anything else once all the components of the bed were in there, which meant that the mattress Dicky had purchased demanded some thought.

Even without the dismantled bed frame filling all

the space in the car, the mattress would not fit inside, of course, so Dicky pulled up on the wide pavement outside the shop, and with the help of the salesman and a long length of rope, which he was expected to return, the new double mattress was tied onto the roof of the little A30, and almost swamped it.

Dicky would have to go slowly and, with the rope fed through the windows to tie it down, be careful that the load did not shift when taking corners.

With rear vision eliminated, as the mattress covered the rear window completely, and with rope tied to the rear bumper, just above the brake lights, and an overhanging portion restricting forward vision, Dicky hoped the vehicle with its unusual load would not attract the attention of the Constabulary.

He also hoped that the grey morning sky did not release the threatened rain until he was safely installed at the flat.

The mattress was wrapped around with a couple of long curtains, which Sophie had declared surplus to requirements, and which Dicky expected to put up across the wide picture window of his new bedroom, when he had time. For now they served to stop the rope cutting into the mattress, and if it should begin to rain, to keep the worst of it off the sleeping surface.

Stepping back and looking at it before he set off,

Dicky decided the little car resembled a sandwich, made with thick white bread.

As the doors were tied shut by the rope, and with assurances from the salesman that he would be fine and had nothing to worry about, he carefully climbed in through the window and started his journey.

After a fair few scary moments and following two stops to tighten the ropes, but otherwise without incident, Dicky turned into Dean Street, about three hundred yards from the flat. There, as he slowly edged up the street, a Traffic Warden popped out, seemingly from nowhere, and signalled for him to pull over.

'What d'you think you are playing at, sonny?' said the robust, not to say fat, little man who approached the car. 'Dangerous that is. You can't drive like that!'

Resisting the temptation to say that he had actually driven all the way from Pinner without a problem, Dicky explained that he was only a few yards from his destination and asked to be allowed to continue.

'I should get a policeman and have you arrested. How far have you driven like that?'

'Oh, only from just down there,' said Dicky, thinking quickly. 'You can actually see the turning into Richmond Mews, where I'm going from here, look …' said Dicky, pointing. 'I live in Richmond Buildings, in a flat.'

The Traffic Warden looked at the building Dicky was indicating and then back at the car.

'Right,' he said, checking his wristwatch, and after a moment of indecision. 'Here's what we are going to do.'

And so it was that Dicky drove at walking pace to the entrance to Richmond Mews with the Traffic Warden trotting alongside with one hand on the mattress.

When Dicky turned into the road, following his instruction to stop, the Warden paused to catch his breath and said, 'Right. You live there?' He pointed and Dicky confirmed that the building they could see was his destination. 'Well you can consider yourself very lucky that I am just about to go off duty, otherwise, although the paperwork would have been tedious, you would have been nicked!'

'Thank you very much, Officer,' said Dicky.

'And you needn't even contemplate doing something as monumentally stupid as this again. Next time you get a notion to move a ruddy great mattress, even just a short distance, get a friend to help you and carry the damn thing down the road, you hear?'

As he pulled onto the slope and prepared to climb out through the window of the car, Dicky noticed Hamish and a slim, fair-haired girl coming out of the door on the other side of the gate, within the car parking area.

Hamish saw him at the same moment and convulsed in laughter at the sight that greeted him.

Now Hamish unlocked the gate from the inside, and once the gate closed behind them, with the little car safely under cover, he managed to get his laughter under control; introduced Annie, and offered to help him get the mattress into the lift.

Annie helped to untie the ropes so that Dicky could get out of the car without climbing through the window. With as much dignity as he could muster, he stood and shook her hand, and said that Hamish had told him all about her, which made her blush comprehensively as only fair-haired girls can.

-oOo-

Exhausted and rather hot, Dicky sat on the edge of the mattress on the freshly reconstructed bed.

The job of putting all the pieces back together again was straight-forward enough, but it had taken him five journeys, backwards and forwards to the car, to get all the bits. That included one lengthy session searching for a bolt which he eventually discovered had rolled under the back seat.

The bed frame was old, but very sturdy and the mattress fitted perfectly, and as Dicky looked around his new room now, he was very pleased with the way things had turned out.

He hoped that when he returned with his clothes and actually moved in tomorrow, the smell of paint would have dissipated, and he stood and pushed the window open a little further to increase the flow of air, just in time to see a flash of lightning and hear a rumble of thunder, as the first drops of rain started to fall.

He hoped it wasn't a bad omen.

-oOo-

If the truth was told, Hamish was actually a little large for the MG Midget they had borrowed, and with the roof up, against the rain, he was finding it cramped and claustrophobic.

Annie, in the passenger seat, seemed quite content, however, and twittered happily in between shopping sessions, checking her notes and the A-Z road map book they had borrowed from Dicky. Hamish was feeling the strain of all this endless shopping.

'It's a good job we met your friend and borrowed his map book; we have been much quicker getting round these places as a result.'

Hamish, who harboured some doubts that Annie's directions always followed the most direct route, merely grunted, as they pulled up outside yet another furniture shop in the trendier part of

Chelsea.

'Cheer up, Hamish,' said Annie. 'This is the last one.'

-oOo-

Camilla arrived exactly on time at the Restaurant 'Le Caprice', and had to wait in the bar area, on her own, for her mother to arrive.

She had much to occupy her mind and had not slept terribly well after hearing noises.

She knew precisely what the noises were, of course, and they started with Annie trying to close her bedroom door quietly and steal along the corridor to Hamish's bedroom. After that she tried not to listen.

This morning, over breakfast, before they left in the car to visit furniture and fabric suppliers, Annie was a little flushed and looked away each time Camilla tried to catch her eye. But, as she was giving little smiles to Hamish, and he was smiling back, she assumed all was well. Good luck to them, she thought, and knowing that their liaison was somehow right, she smiled to herself now.

Her mind turned to why she had been so firmly instructed to come to this restaurant, and she wondered what this imperious summons was all about. That old weasel, Simpkin, had thoroughly enjoyed telling her that her mother was most insistent that she should come, and he made her feel she was a naughty child being told not to disobey.

She had been to 'Le Caprice' before, of course, and noticed that the art deco interior was becoming a little battered around the edges. It was still one of those places where one might come across celebrities, however, which was why it was on her mother's list of places to see and be seen. Her mother was not vain, she decided, or not really, and she knew that her days as one of the glittering film and theatre set were behind her. But she just kept going to the same places because … well, because of what? Because that was what she did. Even in her least charitable thoughts about her mother, Camilla could not find it in her heart to dislike how she carried on. It was just how she was, and everyone else had to fit in around that.

Glancing now out of the window she saw the Bentley drawing up outside and noticed the doorman and head waiter moving towards the entrance to make a fuss of their new guest, just as her mother always expected.

-oOo-

Chapter 21

Surprising plans

With his clothes in the wardrobe, his suit freshly brushed, and the window wide open to let out the last of the clinging new paint smell, Dicky sighed contentedly.

To his surprise, Sophie had actually shed a tear as she waved him off in the car, after breakfast. She had wanted to come and make his bed and so on, but he assured her that the Army had made it a priority to teach their National Servicemen how to make beds, and he would be fine.

With a promise that she and Gerald would come and see him in the new Mini, once they had got used to it, she wished him well and stood on the doorstep as he reversed the Austin onto the road and took his leave.

His first task had been to return the long rope to

the bed shop, and then buy milk, bread and a few essentials, but after that was done, he had spent the rest of the morning arranging his clothes and trying not to make too much noise as David slept on, unaware of his arrival.

Monday, of course, would see him starting work, and he resolved to get an early night in his new bed and relax for the rest of the weekend, to be fresh and ready as the new working week started. He had calculated that it would take him about twenty-five minutes to walk from the flat to his office, and he considered doing the walk this afternoon, to try it out. But he would be armed with his A-Z map book, when Hamish returned it, so he felt as ready as he could be. He decided instead to visit a store he had spotted down the road, where he might be able to purchase tennis shorts and some swimming trunks, ready for his trip to Surrey in just over a week.

-oOo-

'So, what is this all about, Mummy?' asked Camilla, as the waiter departed with their luncheon order. 'Why the royal summons?'

'I thought it would be nice to have lunch on your return from Scotland, so you could tell me all about your adventures ...'

'That's not the way Simpkin put it. According to him I was to show up here promptly on pain of death.'

'Oh, you do exaggerate, Camilla, although ...'

'Although?'

'Although there was something I wanted to speak to you about …'

'Well, I'm here. You have the floor.'

'Thank you dear. I'm not quite sure how to put this or where to start …'

Camilla sighed, she had no patience with guessing games.

'I've found that the best place to start is at the beginning, omitting no detail, however slight, as Sherlock Holmes would say.'

'Yes, dear, very well,' Dame Amelia drew a deep breath. 'Camilla, I have decided to go back to work …'

'What!'

-oOo-

Looking at lighting made some sense, and he realised they must choose appropriate furniture, but Hamish thought he had seen as many versions of 'Clan Campbell Dress Modern' tartan as he could stick.

Annie had explained that the fabric was bright, with white accents, so would lighten up the dimly lit castle when used to cover chairs, and in 'feature panels' in strategic locations on the walls, and he thought that sensible and practical. But why it took visits to the showrooms and offices of six potential suppliers to select the version she liked most, was beyond him.

He also struggled to understand why they were ordering tartan in London, from representatives of huge textile mills in England, rather than in its native Scotland, and he asked Annie to explain that again.

'I thought I had covered that,' she said. 'We are going to need a lot of this cloth and the cozy wee crofts where people think this stuff comes from would take months, years even, to fill the order. These textile mills can copy any pattern and produce material in bulk in days. How do you think fashions get copied and in the shops so quickly after they appear on the cat-walk? It is all done on an industrial scale by these places.'

Hamish, hearing the explanation for the second time, took no comfort from it. He would rather wait for the traditional cottage industries in Scotland to catch up. The fact that that was impractical rather took the romance out of it for him, and after last night, he was feeling romantic. In fact the glow he felt had carried him through the tedious business of all this shopping, although as they entered yet another textile company's showroom, it was beginning to wear thin.

-oOo-

'You are going to have to help me with this, Mummy. When you say, "going back to work," what exactly have you in mind?'

'I need to start by telling you about the visit I had from a charming young man, who was calling to see you, bearing flowers.'

Dame Amelia allowed her soup to become cold as she related the story of how she discovered that the enterprising Dicky was a budding playwright, and the series of coincidences which lead to her reading his unpublished plays.

When she came to explain how Camilla had inspired this discovery, following the minor accident between the Bentley, and what she described as 'his funny little car', Camilla gasped.

She knew immediately who the young man was now, and although their meeting had been brief, they had not been introduced, and she did not even know his name, she had regretted that she was unlikely ever to see him again. She had no idea about his charming gesture, turning up at her home with flowers to see if she had suffered any ill effects from the little crash until this moment, and she found that she was smiling at the prospect of meeting him again.

And then her mother delivered another shock.

'So the nub of the thing is that I have decided to

offer to become a patron, along with Herb Walters, to fund putting the play on, and to appear in it in a modest role myself.
I have gathered together a group of friends who will become involved as investors and Herb and I will be building a company of actors, if the young man agrees to work with us.'

'Good Lord! And you did all this while I was away in Scotland?'

'Yes, dear. He who hesitates is lost, as the expression goes, so I decided to 'look sharp and do it now' as the Americans say.'

'And you are throwing this weekend party to talk him into it?'

'Yes, but I also thought you might rather like to meet him again properly. Such a charming young man.'

Camilla put down the soup spoon she had been holding in mid-air over her bowl for some time as her mother's story came to an end.

'You really are quite remarkable, aren't you Mummy. And, yes, I would like to meet this young man again. I would like that.'

-oOo-

Harry Jarvis was pleased with the news that he was not expected to drive over to Pinner to pick Dicky up next weekend, but he was still concerned about meeting him again.

Harry was many things, but he was not, at heart, in favour of violence, especially against himself. He could not forget Dicky's threats and he resolved to do his best to remain very scarce during the big weekend Dame Amelia was planning.

He had thought about asking for leave to visit some fictitious sickly aunt, but having used that excuse to take two days off to go to the races not long ago, he decided that story was not yet ready for another airing.

He had considered pretending to be ill himself, but decided that Simpkin, the officious and meddling butler, might see through that, and it was not worth the risk.

Eventually he came to the conclusion that with several people invited, so long as he kept out of the way of the guests, there should be enough going on to keep them all busy. And particularly, for reasons he could not understand, as Dicky seemed to be the centre of attention at this gathering, he was rarely likely to be on his own, so it should be easy enough to avoid any one-to-one contact with him where the opportunity for unpleasantness might arise.

Nevertheless, Harry remained restless, and was impatient for this weekend party with all its guests and ever-present danger to be over, so that things could return to normal and he could relax.

-oOo-

Chapter 22

'If music be the food of love ...'

Having purchased a new tie, as well as some tennis shorts and other essentials, Dicky decided to treat himself to a leisurely lunch at the Lyons Corner House on Coventry Street, where for five shillings and ninepence, he enjoyed what the menu referred to as the 'FISHDISH', in capital letters and with no space between the words. It comprised "fresh filleted plaice, golden fried, served with French-fried potatoes, lemon and tartare sauce." After that, he spent a further ninepence on a chocolate eclair, and given the warm day, washed it all down with an iced coffee, which was small, and he thought expensive, at a shilling, and regretted not having the "bottomless pot of coffee" for the same price.

Whistling a popular show tune under his breath, replete and contented after a brisk walk in the park, he returned to the flat. As he pressed the button to call the lift from the lobby, the street door opened, and in walked Camilla.

-oOo-

Glancing out of the scullery window, Rufus Simpkin, the butler, saw the Bentley making stately progress down the drive.

'The old girl is back,' he announced.

'About time too,' said Mrs Childs, the cook. 'I've got to finalise these menus with her today or I shan't have time to get everything ordered in.'

'I shall ask her if you may have an audience when she has had time to settle,' said Simpkin, straightening his waistcoat.

'Blow that, Rufus. I'll scoot down and bump into her in the hall when she comes in …'
'You will do no such thing!' exclaimed Simpkin, scandalised.

'Members of the staff do not 'bump into' their employers in an English country house. We are not in America now, Mrs Childs. I shall approach Dame Amelia and ask when she might be able to see you.'

'Oh, come on. She's not royalty you know … and it's 1963, not 1893. I'll just breeze down and catch her.'

'You will *not*. You will wait here until you are called. Now sit down and I will go and welcome her home.'

But Simpkin's dignified plans were immediately scuppered when the door of the scullery burst open and Dame Amelia herself looked in.

'Ah, I thought I might find you in here. Could I have a word about the menus for next weekend, Mrs Childs?' she said.

-oOo-

Dicky lost his grip on the packages he was clutching and the paper bag holding his new swimming trunks split, causing them to tumble out onto the floor.

'I ... I ...' he spluttered.

'Oh, hello,' said Camilla. 'Here, let me help you with that ... haven't we met before?'

'I ... I ...' said Dicky, now bright red, as Camilla held up his swimming trunks.

'You are the chap in the funny little car that we accidentally bumped, aren't you?'

-oOo-

Possibly one of our most significant contributions to civilisation is the idea of a proper breakfast, somebody wise once said. But what it should comprise was causing some consternation at Holme Hall.

'If you have to have something American, Mrs C,

I suppose cornflakes could be served. But pancakes and maple syrup, and that tomato ketchup on everything, and no traditional haddock kedgeree? The idea!'

'And what, pray, did they serve for breakfast in your day, whenever that was, Rufus.'

'Well, you would expect to see kippers, perhaps black pudding, sausages, bacon and various sorts of eggs, of course. Maybe some cold ham, or any left-over game pie and whatnot. The kedgeree should be made with 'Finnan Haddie' for best results, by the way. And there might be devilled kidneys sometimes; and porridge, of course. And plenty of hot toast and marmalade, and tea and coffee …'

'And you would expect all that laid out on the sideboard for the guests to pick at? No wonder people in domestic service died young!' exclaimed Mrs Childs, shaking her head.

'When the late Mr Barron was a younger man, and when I was in the service of his father, that was what was served. Of course all that was before he married and then lived in America.'

'Was he very fat?'

-oOo-

Earlier, Hamish, Annie and Camilla had been discussing their plans for the next day.

'So, we will meet Heather and Siobhan in The Prince of Wales Pub in New Malden, at about three o'clock. I've looked up the train times …'

'I thought you said one of them was called Moira?' asked Hamish.

'Yes, I mean no,' said Annie. 'Her real name is Siobhan but she chooses to be called Moira.'

'Why?'

'Well, isn't it obvious? Nobody can spell Siobhan, and that matters if you are in the music business.'

'But why are we meeting them in a pub in suburbia?' asked Camilla.

'I thought I told you, Milly darling. Heather and the Heartaches have a booking to play there before they head off to a Working Man's Club somewhere in the north of England,' explained Annie. 'We will be able to catch them for a wee chat after they finish their lunchtime set, when the pub shuts.'

-oOo-

Camilla was thinking about that conversation and the shock revelations her mother had made over lunch as she got back to the flat.

It was fun to be involved in Annie's plans, and Hamish was very nice, but she did worry whether this open-air music event they had dreamed up was really such a good idea. And she wondered if it would just fizzle out like so many plans and schemes did, when the complexities of organising it all were considered.

The concept of putting on a play, with all her mother's contacts, was much simpler to grasp however, and the story of the young man turning up with flowers after the accident had touched her romantic nature.

It was nevertheless a considerable shock to find herself unexpectedly face to face with the young man in question now, in the lobby of the building where she lived.

-oOo-

'Are you visiting or a resident here?' Camilla asked, as the lift doors opened.

'I ... I ...' sputtered Dicky.

'Gosh. It *is* a surprise to meet you like this. And I wonder if you could tell me your name. I have placed you correctly, haven't I? The car accident?'

'I ... I ...' said Dicky.

'Camilla Barron-Zukor,' she said, holding out her hand. 'My friends call me Milly.'

Dicky finally managed to get his tongue under control enough to splutter out a sentence.

'Very nice to meet you. I'm Dicky.'

'Yes, of course you are. I remember now, your wife referred to you by that name ...'

'My wife?' Dicky looked confused. 'No, my sister, the owner of the car ...'

'Well, that's cleared that up,' said Camilla, under her breath. 'Was her little car very badly damaged?' she asked.

'Er, it's my car now. My sister sold it to me after the accident.'

'Oh,' said Camilla.

'And no, it was just a dent. Another dent, I mean. There are plenty on the car already.'

'I thought it was so sweet of you to call to see if I was all right after the bump, and to deliver flowers. I'm sorry I wasn't there to receive them myself. Thank you very much,' Camilla gave a broad smile which left Dicky devastated. 'So this play you have written ...'

'My ... my play?'

'My mother has told me all about it. She must really believe in it to get behind it so comprehensively ...'

Dicky, of course, was completely unaware of Dame Amelia's plans for the play. He knew she had read both his scripts and might introduce him to someone who could help him at the weekend she was planning, but that was all. So now he received the second major surprise he was to encounter today.

'Putting any play on is a huge risk and a considerable financial investment of course. But it is time Mummy got involved in something new again, and if she throws herself into this with her usual vigour and determination, I'm sure she will do your play justice.'

As the lift doors decided nobody was taking any notice of them and closed again with moody clunk, Dicky was standing on one leg with his mouth open, staring at Camilla in confusion.

'I say, are you all right?' she said.

-oOo-

Chapter 23

'An enticing prospect'

There was a blackboard leaning against the wall of The Prince of Wales, just down the road from the station in New Malden, and it proclaimed that 'Heather and the Heartaches' would be playing here at lunchtime followed by 'The Roosters' this evening.

They had to knock on the locked door to attract attention when they arrived, and were eventually admitted by a sweating, paunchy man in an apron, who having asked what they wanted in a gruff voice, allowed them in to the noisy bar area where a group of young men were practising on guitars and other instruments, and in a corner, Heather and Moira sat with what looked like accounts ledgers open on a table.

As they shook hands and introduced themselves,

shouting above the noise, Ally, another member of the band, came over.

'Their guitarist is good,' said Ally. 'But I suggested he come up with a stage name, like we all did. I told him he would never get far with a dopey name like Eric.'

'I've no intention of changing my name,' said Heather. 'I've always been Heather and I always will.'

'Is there nowhere quieter we can go?' asked Hamish. 'Yon noise is fair splitting ma eardrums!'

As he spoke, the sweating publican appeared, and tapping his wristwatch, approached the practising band, who stopped playing and began packing up their equipment.

'Pity, I was enjoying that,' said Moira. 'I would have liked to see them play tonight, but we will be in the van again on the way to … where was it again?'

'Worksop,' said Heather. 'I wrote it down for you on a wee bit of paper tay put in the right page in the map book.'

'I'm Ally, by the way,' said Ally, 'seeing as nobody seems to want to introduce me. I play bass guitar.'

-oOo-

Dicky simply could not believe what had just happened. He had told David the story three times now, and was still finding it impossible to sit down.

"Who ever loved that loved not at first sight?" (As You Like It – Act 3, Scene 5),' said David, tellingly.

'Honestly, David,' said Dicky. 'I'm a pretty straightforward, maybe even boring sort of a chap, but this girl has absolutely knocked me for a loop. I can't wait to see her again.'

'Delightful,' said David. 'And have you made another date, or are you going to be haunting the lobby, in case she wants you to call the lift again?'

-oOo-

'I cannae see that catching on,' said Heather. 'It's bladdy remote where yon castle is, Annie, and the weather is more often dreich than not. Do you really see folk wanting tae pay good money tae listen to bands in the rain on yon bleak hillside?'

'You may have a point there,' said Camilla.

'It might be fine in, where did you say it was? Richmond-on-Thames in London. Aye, that was it; Fine there tae have one of these outdoor jam sessions, but in the Highlands? I cannae see it,' said Moira.

'I was worried, ...' began Hamish.

'Ah, no, but I think you are missing the point. What was Gary telling us about the other day, Ally?' said Heather.

'Where Gary's parents worked, y'mean?' asked Ally.

'Aye, that's it. And here he comes now, bless him. Gary, this is Milly and Annie and Hamish. They have got a castle in the Highlands and some daft wee ideas tae make money outta it.'

'Tell us about where your dad worked when you were a kid, Gary,' said Moira.

Gary was painfully shy at the best of times, and now he had all these people looking at him expecting him to speak, he wished he was back with his guitar, jamming with the Roosters and that Eric bloke, who he really seemed to connect with.

'C'mon laddie,' said Moira. 'These folks won't bite. Tell us about that place your father worked in, down in Wales.'

'You ...you mean the holiday camp?' he managed.

'If that was what it was called, yes,' said Heather.

'Gary was telling me the Queen and the Duke of Edinburgh are due to go there for an official visit in August ...' said Ally.

'Erm, you mean Butlin's in Pwllheli in Wales, do you?' said Gary.

'That's it,' said Heather. 'Tell us about it.'

'Well, my da worked there as a Redcoat. That was before we moved to Scotland, of course. What do you want to know about it?'

'What was it like? said Camilla.

'Well, Pwllheli was more or less invisible,' said Gary, 'But Billy Butlin sort of put it on the map.'

'Come on, laddie, don't be shy, I want tae hear aboot this place,' said Hamish.

'Well, when I was little, there was a lot of holidaymakers and the Butlin's Redcoats, of course. And a big dining hall and entertainments room, where they had dances and the Redcoats put on shows. There was also a swimming pool, and a sports field, where they had embarrassing three-legged and egg and spoon races. For grown up people, mark you. And they had a donkey derby, that my da made me help with.'

'Go on,' said Camilla, intrigued.

'I was only about twelve or thirteen when we moved on, but I do remember they were building a funfair sort of thing, and some more permanent wooden chalets there, when we left. There was also table tennis and snooker tables, and coin-in-the-slot machines, which were all right from my point of view. But the worst bit was the early morning wake-up-call. Hated that, I did.'

'And people paid to have their holidays there?' asked Hamish, who could see the germ of an idea forming. This, or something like it, might just create an opportunity for the castle and grounds, and might have more long term potential than just a single music event, he thought.

-oOo-

There was a wide stone bench in the compact garden behind the offices and flats, and a discreet door, almost hidden behind the lift shaft and stairs, that allowed visitors to make use of it.

Although invited, Camilla thought she might be in the way while Hamish took Annie out for an early supper on their return from New Malden, so she used the opportunity to explore this little garden, which she had been meaning to look at for some time.

There, to her delight, she found she had been joined by a cat who sat on the bench, and through some sort of telepathy, seemed to Camilla to be inviting her to sit with him.

Camilla liked cats and, needing no further invitation, promptly sat down and began stroking, in just the right place, behind the right ear.

Since the days of 'Inky Thunderfoot', there had never been a cat like Sid in all the W1 postal districts of London, and his dominance and prowess at dispatching mice, (and possibly rats, although no evidence had been found to support that claim) was unequalled.

His superiority shone through in his confident manner, and although he had allowed himself to purr to encourage Camilla to keep up the treatment, he was dignified and self-assured.

Not, it must be said, that he was the handsomest of cats, and his expression tended more towards the scowl than anything else. But Sid could not help that, and usually overcame this setback with a series of well-practised and charming gestures when he wanted to make friends. He found Camilla an attractive and indulgent companion and soon took up a new position, on her lap, to better receive her attentions.

When Dicky glanced out of the window of his bedroom and saw Camilla fussing the cat in the little garden, he almost fell over himself in his rush to get down the stairs to join them.

-oOo-

'Well, I'm thinking it might be just the thing,' Hamish was saying, as he sprinkled salt on his chips. 'And it needn't cost the earth tae set it up. Just a few tents tae start with ...'

'And it would't have to be so ... so common as that Butlin's place,' added Annie. 'We could make it appeal to more a more discerning clientele. Hikers, y'ken, and those coming for the fishing; or shooting parties.'

'Aye, but with stuff for the wives and kiddies tae do while the blokes are off doing that. And there is already the big banqueting hall for entertainments. There is plenty room for a bar in there. I wonder how much it would cost tae dig a swimming pool ...'

'It would need to be an indoor sort of pool, because of the weather.'

'Yes, good point. That might run tae money.'

'But then we could open it all year round ...'

'We?'

'Well, it occurred tae me that you might need an assistant ...'

-oOo-

'Oh, hello again,' said Camilla.

'Oh, ah. Yes, hi,' blustered Dicky. 'I see you have met Sid. Everyone likes him. Except David, my flatmate, that is.'

'He doesn't like cats?'

'Well, yes. I mean he might, but he is horribly allergic to them, you see,' Dicky tried what he thought might be a sympathetic smile. 'Sid makes his eyes water and sets him off sneezing, so he is not allowed in our flat.'

'Oh, poor Sid. I'm sure he doesn't mean any harm,'

smiled Camilla, as the cat settled more comfortably on her lap. 'Who does he belong to?'

'Belong to? Oh, I see what you mean,' Dicky thought for a moment before he replied. 'Well, I'm not sure he belongs to anyone, actually. As you probably know it's all offices round here, in terms of immediate area, I mean …'

'Do you think he might be a stray?'

'I suppose he might be, but he looks quite well cared for.'

'Perhaps. But I shall put food out for him here, in this garden, from now on. At least until we find out who owns him. I couldn't bear to think that he was lost and going hungry.'

This girl has a kindly soul, loves animals, and is prepared to put herself out to help others. Was it possible that she could be any more perfect, thought Dicky.

'Erm, speaking of being hungry …'

'Pardon?'

'Er, eating, I mean … have you had any supper?'

'I wondered when he might get round to that,' whispered Camilla into Sid's ever attentive ear. 'No, as it happens, I was just thinking about getting myself something …' she said.

'Well, I mean to say. That is, may I ... would you like to join me ... There is a restaurant ... Completely understood if you would rather not, or have other plans, of course ...'

'No, no plans. I should like to go to a restaurant with you for supper. Thank you very much.'

Recognising his cue, Sid hopped down from her lap, yawned and stretched, and with a swish of his tail to indicate satisfaction at a job well done, he strolled off towards the opening in the hedge that he used as his personal entrance to this garden.

-oOo-

Chapter 24

And so the work begins

The 'quiet day' Dicky had promised himself to prepare for starting his new job had turned out to be rather busy and momentous, especially at its end, over dinner.

Camilla had been charming, and effortlessly guided their conversation until almost all of his nervousness left him, and he found himself relaxing in her company.

When they touched on the subject of the next weekend, when he was to attend the gathering at her mother's house, he did feel the muscles of his stomach tighten slightly, but Camilla assured him that there would be very little formality and that Dame Amelia was an excellent hostess.

She explained that her mother was born to a modest

family in London, and got into the big time in movies when she married Aaron Zukor, second son of the founder of Paramount Pictures in America, but the marriage didn't last, and a few years later she married Camilla's father, who came from an old English family, with Holme Hall as their family seat.

Life there, since her mother returned from America, had been quite relaxed, and although they still retained the butler and other staff, there was no stiff old fashioned ceremony, and she said she was sure Dicky would be made to feel most welcome.

Those stomach muscles tightened again now, however, as he approached the offices of Sigsmund Publications, where his new working life was about to begin.

-oOo-

A little after nine, and having received expressions of gratitude for her hospitality, Camilla saw her guests into their taxi to catch their train back to Scotland.

She returned to her flat, and prepared to wash up after the breakfast she had prepared for them, to send them on their way.

As she turned on the hot water she glanced out of the kitchen window which overlooked the little garden, and smiled as she noticed Sid, tucking into the morsel of left-over sausage she had placed for him beside the bench.

'I hope you approve,' she said. 'That is a little thank you for yesterday. You might like to know our date went very well, although you may consider me a little forward when I tell you that I kissed him on the cheek, when he saw me to my door.'

Having disposed of the sausage, Sid glanced up at the windows of the building and Camilla may have imagined it, but she thought he caught her eye. Then, as cats will, he began the engrossing business of washing his paws.

-o0o-

Samuel P. Sigsmund and Captain E. Wilson greeted Dicky, as he was shown once more into the office where he had his interview.

After welcoming him and explaining the routines for tea breaks and so on, Captain Wilson took him on a tour of the offices. It did not take long as the area the company occupied on the third floor of the building only comprised five or six rooms.

Other than Mr Sigsmund's office, those he had been shown so far were all plainly decorated with utilitarian furniture, and Dicky was shown a desk with a typewriter that was for his use when he was in the office.

'Of course,' said Captain Wilson. 'You probably won't be spending very much time here at all, as most of your time will be spent out and about reviewing the various shows and so forth. These desks are just used to type up copy mostly, before it goes to the editors and then the compositor to be put in the magazines.'

'I see,' said Dicky.

'There are two editors who will accept your copy, alongside myself as managing editor. I'll take you to meet them now.'

Down a short corridor two glazed doors faced each other and Captain Wilson knocked once and opened the door on the left.

Through the haze of cigarette smoke, Dicky could make out two immensely untidy desks, both with typewriters and telephones and occupied by a balding harassed looking man in glasses and a slim older woman in tweeds.

'May I introduce Cyril Jenkins, our Features Editor and Miss Pinewood, his secretary.'

Shaking hands, Dicky very much wanted to cough as the airless fog of the office cut across his throat, but realising that might be regarded as rude he resisted the urge.

'Good grief, Cyril,' Captain Wilson was saying. 'Don't you ever open a window in here, Miss Pinewood will be getting kippered!'

'Miss Pinewood has given up smoking,' smiled Cyril,

removing the cigarette from the corner of his mouth. 'The smoke in here helps her to deal with the craving.'

On the other side of the corridor, Captain Wilson knocked and opened the door of an identical and equally untidy office, that was mercifully smoke-free. It differed only from the other room in that one wall was crammed floor to ceiling with bookcases, overflowing with books and magazines of all descriptions.

At one of the desks a solid-looking girl sat typing, but the other desk was unoccupied.

'Is Mr Peters not in, Gloria?' Captain Wilson enquired.

'Not yet Captain, train strikes.'

'Ah, yes, of course, that would explain it. Dicky, this is Gloria Eastman, secretary to Mr Peters and our archivist. Gloria, would you ask Mr Peters to step into my office when he arrives so that I can introduce him to our new member of staff.'

Without further ado Captain Wilson led the way to his own office, which was every bit as large and elegantly decorated as that of Samuel P. Sigsmund, but it looked to the rear of the building, rather than across the gardens in the square.

Captain Wilson waved Dicky to a seat and picked up one of two telephones to speak to Cynthia, the receptionist, and request some tea.

'So, Dicky. Do you have any questions?'

'Yes,' said Dicky. 'I wonder if you might explain the relationship between advertising in the magazines and the reviews that you publish, please.'

'Aha! Straight to the nub of the delicate balance our business must maintain, Dicky. I like that in a journalist. No beating about the bush, what!'

-oOo-

When Dicky put his key in the lock of the flat after his first day at the office, the telephone was ringing, and he rushed to answer it.

It was his sister Sophie, calling from the telephone box at the end of her road, and she was anxious to learn how his first day in his new job went.

After Dicky thanked her for her concern and told her the edited highlights of his day, Sophie had news to impart too.

'Well, you will be pleased to hear that all the furniture and stuff from Gerald's mum's house was sold in the auction, and it raised quite a good price. More than we expected actually.'

'I'm delighted to hear that. It was all of quite good quality, I thought, and my bed is quite comfortable. I hope the fact that I pinched it out of the collection didn't hold back the rest of the sale items ...'

'Oh, no, Dicky, quite the opposite. The man from the auction house said beds don't sell and it might actually have held back the other stuff, so in a way you did us a favour.'

'Well, that's good. And how are you getting on with the new Mini?'

'Oh, Dicky, it's wonderful! It gets admiring glances wherever we go, and it is really fast … compared to Petal, I mean.'

'And no doubt, by now, you have thought of a name to give it, Sis.'

'Of course. It is called "Duo" because it has two colours of paint, and is my constant companion. We are rarely seen apart … hence "Duo" seemed appropriate. The car is the other half of the duo, you see.'

'I see,' said Dicky, who had suddenly become aware that in his haste to answer the ringing telephone, he had not closed the front door. As he looked towards it he noticed that Camilla was in the doorway, looking adorable in a short, cotton voile dress and strappy cork-heeled sandals. She was leaning nonchalantly on the door frame with one foot resting on the woodwork, and examining her nails.

'Er, I have to go now, Sis. Visitors. I'll come and see you next week sometime.'

-oOo-

At last the long train journey up to Scotland was coming to an end.

For Hamish and Annie, however, the time seemed to flash by as they sat close together with one of Annie's sketchpads, making notes and writing down ideas relating to the 'luxury holiday and activity camp' they were keenly planning.

'Och, I'm sure Uncle Jock is going tae love this,' said Hamish, not for the first time.

'Hamish, you keep saying that. Of course he will,' smiled Annie, snuggling a little closer to him. 'But I bet he has already guessed that I love you.'

'Oh, Annie,' sighed Hamish. 'I wish we were no on this confounded train, so I could kiss ye properly.'

'You are always so proper, Hamish. I don't care who is looking, but if you are shy, put my wee coat over our heads and get on with it!'

'Och, gurrl. Have ye no shame?' said Hamish pulling the coat up over his head and drawing Annie towards him.

-oOo-

In calling to see how Dickie's first day in his new job went, Camilla had an entirely alternative motive.

She had no food in the house, after the breakfast she

had provided for Hamish and Annie, and she knew she must go shopping, but she had put it off when an idea occurred to her.

'So these days people go Dutch all the time, sharing the bill in restaurants and whatever. It is commonplace in America, where I grew up, and if you won't let me even up the score by buying you dinner tonight, we can do that, if you insist,' laughed Camilla. 'But if your pride won't let you even consider going Dutch, then you condemn me to starvation this evening as I have nothing in my flat to eat at all, and most of the shops will be shut by now.'

'It looks like you have been cornered, Dickie, old man, either that or "The lady doth protest too much, methinks" (Hamlet, Act 3, Scene 2),' said David, appearing from the bathroom in his dressing gown. 'I'd join you myself, if you were going Dutch, but I rather think I might be in the way ...'

'Oh no, David, you would be most welcome to join us, of course. Or maybe, if
Dicky here doesn't want to come out to play, perhaps just you and I could go?'

'Erm ...' said Dicky. 'That will be all right. David has to work, so dinner is on me Camilla, and Dutch if you like, although ...'

'Dutch it is then. You may call for me at half past seven,' and blowing him a kiss, Camilla skipped back into her own flat and closed the door.

'I need to talk to you, David' said Dicky as he closed their own flat door.

'Looks like things are turning out well there, Dicky, my boy!' said David. 'Now what was this thing you wanted to talk to me about …If it's about the birds and the bees…'

'No, David. It is actually a deadly serious matter and it concerns you directly.'

'Ooo, dear! Was it something I said?' fluttered David.

-oOo-

Chapter 25

Unexpected consequences

'So there it is, David. I have to do 'The Mousetrap' at the Ambassadors Theatre, and Mr Peters will do 'My Fair Lady' at the Theatre Royal'.'

'So the idea is to see how they have stood the test of time and review them back to back, as they are now, then?'

'Yes, that is the plan. 'The Mousetrap' has been on since November 1952, you know …'

'And 'My Fair Lady' had been running since 1958. Yes, I know. Are you expected to do a hatchet job on them?'

'I don't think so. Mr Peters just told me to write an in-depth review, he didn't give me any steer as to how to present it,' said Dicky.

'You know 'My Fair Lady' is due to have the financial people in to do an audit, and we are all dreading that. I can't say we have been exactly packing them in lately, and if your Mr Peters sees that ...'

'Thank goodness that he gave me 'The Mousetrap' to do,' said Dicky. 'I wouldn't have wanted to do to anything to harm ...'

'You don't have to say it,' said David, who was fighting back tears. 'It's your job. Nothing personal, I know that. I don't suppose you could let me know when he is coming so I can warn the cast ... oh, good grief! Forget I said that! That was completely wrong!'

'I could tip you off ...'

'No, absolutely not. That would be unforgivably dishonest. And if this Mr Peters found out, you would be out of a job before your bum had so much as warmed your chair.'

'You are probably right.'

'Of course I'm right. Theatres and theatrical people thrive on rumours, leaks and tittle-tattle, it would be impossible to keep a thing like that secret. In fact you shouldn't really have told me at all ...'

'But I thought ...'

'I know you did, bless you. But it is no good, there is nothing whatsoever we can do about it. If this Peters destroys us, knowing it is coming won't help anyone.'

'I suppose not …'

'Look,' said David, blowing his nose, 'you go and get ready for this Dutch-style date of yours. If you don't leave a ring round the tub, like the previous Sebastian, we shall remain friends, and we shall forget all about this. That would be best.'

And after squeezing Dicky's arm, David dived into his bedroom and shut the door.

-o0o-

The cozy restaurant Dicky and Camilla chose for supper was quiet, and they were offered a table in a little bay screened on two sides from the rest of the diners.

'So tomorrow I will be off down to Surrey to help mother prepare for the weekend house party,' Camilla was saying. 'Although what precisely I shall be expected to do, I have no idea.'

'What would you like to do?' asked Dicky.

'Well, if it was up to me, which it won't be of course, I would like to help Mrs Childs, the cook, in the kitchen. She will have masses to do and I love to cook.'

'Your mother has a cook?'

'Yes, mother imported her from America, much

to the chagrin of the butler who likes everything traditional and runs a mile at the sight of a ketchup bottle.'

'So there is a butler and a chauffeur, both of whom I have encountered, and a cook. That's quite a household to support.'

'To support one aging actress, you mean? But we haven't finished yet. In no particular order there is an estate manager, a footman, and two, or is it three, maids. Most of them came with the house when mummy married my father. Then there are the tenant farmers, of course, I forgot them. My father's family have all lived in The Hall, and its predecessor which burned down in the eighteen-somethings. We go back for generations so the story goes. But Daddy scandalised them all by marrying an actress and moving to America, of all places.'

'I thought you said you grew up there.'

'I did, although mostly I was shuffled off to a succession of boarding schools, colleges and finally university in England, so I didn't spend much time there. Mummy was moving about with various shows and quite a bit of film work most of the time, so I was probably rather in the way.'

'What about your father ...'

'Daddy flitted back to London from time to time to show his face and attend to the family business, and he made time to come and see me whenever he could, but he died when I was fifteen and at Roedean, down in Sussex ...'

'Oh, I'm sorry ...' said Dicky.

'Thank you. So was I. I thought I would never get over it, but then Mummy did something remarkable. She walked away from the very successful play she was in, tore up a film contract and moved back to England, where she wrapped me in a sort of protective bubble as she tried to establish herself as a member of the English aristocracy, and run Holme Hall as daddy's ancestors would have liked.'

After their meal, as Dicky paused on Camilla's doorstep, she had instructions for him.

'Now, I've put some bags of Spratt's Dry Cat Food under the stairs with a bowl, for you to put out for Sid on your way home each evening, and I want you to ask David to do it while you are down in Surrey. I know he says he is allergic to cats, but he only has to pour some into the bowl and put it out under the bench, so he won't have to get too close.'

'But ...'

'I can't bear to think of Sid going hungry while I'm not around to look after him, and I'm depending on you boys to keep an eye on him while I'm away.'

'Right-ho,' said Dicky, unconvinced, but quite prepared to do anything to please this wonderful girl. 'I'll say good night then ...'

'There is one other thing I wanted to say,' Camilla reached out and took Dicky's hand. 'When you have to go and do your reviews of all these plays and shows, if you wanted any company ...'

'Oh, yes please!' said Dicky.

-oOo-

Agatha Christie's 'The Mousetrap' is the longest running show, of any kind, in the world. It opened in November 1952 at The Ambassadors Theatre in London, and now Dicky had to review it for a feature on how long-running plays in the West End had stood the test of time.

He asked Mr Peters, a long, thin unsmiling man with adenoids, how he should approach the task, and was told that fifteen hundred words would be sufficient, but that was all.

He asked Captain Wilson if he had any advice on the tone required or what background research he should do, and was told to read some previous reviews and establish if there had been many recent cast changes, which could indicate a show was in difficulty, but otherwise just to write about what he saw and give his honest opinion of the show.

As he sat down with a pile of previous editions of the magazine and some newspaper cuttings Gloria Eastman found for him, he was uncomfortable, but at least he would be well read on the history of the play.

It would have been better if Camilla could have come with him to help as a 'sounding board' but she had left early that morning for Surrey, and with a ticket for tonight's performance in his pocket, Dicky was on his own.

-oOo-

Uncle Jock nodded sagely.

The old byre would need some work, particularly to the roof, but it was in the ideal location for a toilet block, and with a modest extension, could accommodate showers as well.

'Yon lassie had got a bee in her bonnet, I'm thinking,' he said quietly to Hamish, as he watched Annie taking measurements and drawing on a pad of graph paper.

'She agrees wi' me that the camping idea is the best, ye ken.'

'Aye,' Uncle Jock nodded once more. 'But ah meant about you, young Hamish. Have ye asked her to marry you yet?'

-oOo-

Chapter 26

An awkward moment

Dicky had thoroughly enjoyed the 'The Mousetrap', and with the exception of one minor incident, where a new member of the cast briefly fluffed his lines, the performance was flawless.

He found writing the required fifteen-hundred words easy, and could have produced more, in what amounted to a glowing review. Yet he was uneasy as he knocked on Mr Peter's door to hand it in, and enquire how he had got on at 'My Fair Lady'.

'Thank you, Dicky,' said the unsmiling Mr Peters, as he handed over his typed pages, but before Dicky could ask about how the other show went, he had more to say. 'Now Gloria has all the details and some of the tickets for you for two new plays and a musical I want you to review this week. Two are in London and one is in Wimbledon, so I think you will have to be prepared to go to a matinee of one of them to get it all done in time.'

Gloria heaved herself up from her desk and handed Dicky a thick, brown foolscap- size envelope containing details of the shows.

'I couldn't get tickets of the Wimbledon one for you, so will have to leave that to you, but I have got as much information together on the other two as I can. They are bigger shows, of course so are being better promoted, but the Wimbledon one is from a new theatre company that sounds quite interesting.'

'I see,' said Dicky, accepting the package. 'Do you know much about them?'

'Not really, except that they have some quite high profile backers, with a history, at least in the past, of launching some very successful shows. I've put a bit of background in there about Sir Herbert Walters who runs the business behind this new play in Wimbledon and may be bankrolling it.'

'Can you organise some tea, in Captain Wilson's office, please Gloria. I have a meeting there in ten minutes,' said Mr Peters.

'Thanks, Gloria. Any idea what it is about?' said Dicky, on his way through the door.

'It is a comedy, set in wartime England, I think. The information is all in there.'

'Right-ho,' said Dicky, as Gloria bustled past him on her way to the kitchen.

Dicky returned to his desk with his envelope to study his next appointments.

-oOo-

John Cohen had worked for the manufacturer, Ace Caravans, for several years, but now that his father considered he had served his apprenticeship, he joined the family firm as a salesman in their established secondhand caravan dealership, 'North Circular Caravans and Camping Supplies'.

John's training had, of course, been interrupted by National Service, which is where he had met Hamish Swinney. That stood him in good stead now, when Hamish remembered their acquaintance and contacted the company to enquire about the purchase of some tents.

'I ain't sure you have thought this through,' John said now. 'If this is meant to be what you might call a more sophisticated camping operation, aimed at the shooting and fishing set, would they really want to be roughing it in tents? Even in Butlin's you get a shed, which they call a chalet, to sleep in.'

'Well,' Hamish started to say.

'No, what you want, Hamish, my old son, is touring caravans. Much more comfortable, and it so 'appens that I can put you right, with second-hand stock that we have available right now, or coming in at the end of the season.'

'I don't know …' Hamish wavered.

'If you are worried about budget, let me reassure you. I can let you have three secondhand Eccles Alerts straight away for more or less the same price that you would pay for the equivalent four-man tents, new.'

'Really?' said Hamish.

'Yes, and each sleeps four and has the advantage that you can wheel them around to mow the grass under them and that sort of thing. They even have a gas ring to have a brew, and gas lighting. Much more civilised.'

Hamish knew nothing about the world of caravans, but it occurred to him that those John was offering might not be very new.

'How old are these, John?' he asked.

'The Eccles Alert was made between 1948 and 1955, and it is not easy to say exactly when each of our three was made, but I can assure you they are all in excellent condition 'aving been well maintained in our own workshops. No leaks, recently painted, nothing to worry about at all. And if you was 'appy with them we will 'ave a Berkeley Argosy coming in soon, and I know where I can get my 'ands on two big luxury Bluebird Sunparlours what sleeps six, I think, and they have proper kitchens with gas cookers and all.'

'But won't that cost a fortune?'

'Nah, not for a mate, Hamish. And we can even arrange to get them delivered to you, if you like. Your campsite business could be up and running pretty much straight away!'

'Well that does sound very tempting ...' said Hamish.

-oOo-

The musical Dicky had been sent to review was 'Half a Sixpence' staring Tommy Steele. The plot revolved around a cockney shop clerk who inherits money and is torn between his childhood sweetheart and society, and the story is based on the book 'Kipps' by H. G. Wells.

Dicky found the stage show well-written and presented, and the songs entertaining. 'Half a Sixpence', he explained in his review, is a lighthearted, rags-to-riches affair, and is none the worse for the fact that it was designed around teenage heartthrob Tommy Steele.

The next review for a matinee performance was a different matter. 'My Wedding Bells?' failed to grip and Dicky was forced to suggest that it would not be around for very long on the West End stage. It had opened on Broadway in New York in 1961 to mixed reviews, and Dicky found it hard to say much good about it.

Dicky found, however, that he was incensed by the play he went to see next.

In Wimbledon, having purchased his ticket at the door of the theatre he found himself watching an account of the plight of National Servicemen and their relationships with the Army Regulars they encountered. Set at end of the war and the beginning of the modern and most recent form of National Service, it made out that National Servicemen were regarded as second-class citizens and seen as layabouts who just wanted to have parties and chase girls, by the Regulars.

Dicky knew what it was like to receive just under forty shillings a week, when the average wage for civilians was about fifteen pounds. There was no money for having fun, and sometimes the low wages were reduced still further by deductions for lost or damaged kit and equipment. In his experience National Servicemen often had little money left for any social activities beyond a visit to the Navy, Army and Air Force Institutes, or NAAFI, as it was known.

From his own very recent experience, he knew that the stance the play took was not a true reflection of what he had been through, and found it deeply inaccurate and offensive both to National Servicemen and to the Regulars whom it sought to pitch as somehow superior and dismissive of their conscripted colleagues.

'Not Real Soldiers' was also badly let down by several instances of lines being forgotten and long silences while waiting for prompts, and while most of the young cast did their best to pull it off, it was pretty obvious that even the older actors who the theatre named in the programme as the 'stars' were somewhat under-rehearsed.

But it was the subject matter that offended Dicky, and the next day he drove to his office to deliver his copy and also to seek out his favourite Traffic Warden.

Former Sergeant Ernest Bacon was previously a Regular in the British Army, and Dicky wanted to see him to check his facts and make sure that his view of relations between the two types of servicemen was not unique.

Dicky knew that National Service, introduced in 1947 to overcome military manpower shortages in the wake of the Second World War (1939-45), had elongated wartime conscription which was extended into an obligatory period of National Service for men of military age. More than two million were called up to the armed forces, often serving in one of Britain's many garrisons around the world.

After attending a medical and joining up, Dicky had six weeks of basic training to get used to military life.

Once enlisted and inside 'camp', National Servicemen like him were issued with their equipment, comprising a uniform (which often didn't fit) and boots. They were then 'knocked into shape', sometimes none too gently, by sergeants under pressure to train them in as short a time as possible.

It was usual for recruits to immediately begin the seemingly endless polishing of kit and equipment. Many regarded this as a mindless drill aimed at destroying individuality, but Dicky soon came to understand that this strict regime helped to foster a group identity, even if it fermented some resentment in attitudes to their superiors, and it served to bring the recruits closer together.

There were opportunities to learn new skills available, and Dicky, as one of the 'other ranks' was trained in general clerical duties, such as typing, whilst some of his colleagues received more specific training in technical subjects, including communications and engineering. Although Dicky stuck to typing and clerical work, he could have learnt languages - especially Russian as the 'Cold War' period rolled on - at the Joint Service School of Languages at Bodmin.

Although, by luck, he was not posted anywhere too dangerous, for those deployed to a war zone, the possibility of death or injury was a very real part of daily life. Many men had of been thrust into combat situations, in Korea, Malaya and Suez, and with minimal training they were expected to fight guerrillas or cope with riots or civil war situations. There was no time for parties and no money for luxuries for any of them.

Dicky knew that between 1947 and 1963, a total of three-hundred and ninety-five National Servicemen were killed on active service, yet this play sought to make out that they were cosseted playboys who had the time of their lives while 'real soldiers' did all the work and took all the risks.

Dicky had also seen how new bonds formed quickly between men from disparate backgrounds, thrown together in a strange situation. He knew that some of the friendships formed during National Service, such as his own with Hamish Swinney, would last a lifetime.

Dicky was driven now by a sense of righteous indignation, and having failed to find Sgt. Bacon on duty in the London square where he parked and they first met, he found a telephone box and put in a call to him at his home as soon as he was able.

Mrs Bacon, who answered the telephone, informed Dicky that her husband was due back at any moment, and if he called again in half an hour, he was bound to find him in.

Dicky used the time to deliver his other two reviews, and then asked Gloria for permission to use the office telephone to call Sgt. Bacon, explaining that, before he submitted his third review, he wanted to check some facts with an old colleague.

-oOo-

Camilla was kept busy preparing Holme Hall for their guests.

Her mother asked her to offer to help Simpkin, the butler, with tasks such as making beds and so on, but he recoiled from the thought.

'That would not be seemly, Miss Camilla,' he said. 'Perhaps you would like to help me to conduct a tour of the house to establish which room will be offered to which guest, instead? Dame Amelia has left that task to me, of course, but it would be useful to have your approval of what I propose. And then, if there is time, I would appreciate your help to carry out an inspection of the reception and dining rooms to ensure that the cleaning has been adequately undertaken ...'

'And *then* can I go and help Mrs Childs in the kitchen?' asked Camilla petulantly.

'If you would like to, Miss Camilla, although I'm sure Mrs Childs has matters well in hand by this late stage. The first of the guests will be arriving tomorrow, after all.'

-oOo-

The very first of those guests to arrive was Sir Herbert 'Herb' Walters, the well-known theatre impresario and former Hollywood film producer.

With all due ceremony Simpkin showed him through to the library.

'I will inform Dame Amelia that you have arrived and have your bags taken to your room, sir. I trust you will find the Blue Room Suite to your liking.'

'I'm sure it will be just grand, thank you.'

'While you are waiting, sir, you may like to know that the papers and periodicals have just been delivered. I have arranged them on that table. I thought you might particularly be interested to glance at the new edition of 'The Critical Review' or perhaps "Theatre and Cinema News', incorporating 'Box Office', which has just gone on sale.'

As Dame Amelia arrived at the library, some minutes later, her guest was leafing through the pages of 'The Critical Review', and let out a little cry as he finished reading one particular article.

'Are you all right, Herb?' asked Dame Amelia solicitously.

'Yes …Yes, thank you, Amelia. Although I have just

had a bit of a shock.'

'A shock?'

'Yes. This review of 'Not Real Soldiers'... it is a play I'm involved in that has just opened ...'

'Not good?'

'Disastrous!'

'Oh, dear, let me see ...'

Sir Herbert passed the magazine across.

'I've not come across that reviewer before, although I can't think why, but his name seems familiar,' he added. 'Who is this Richard Bourne? He has absolutely slated 'Not Real Soldiers' ...'

-oOo-

'Oh, Lordy. I'm so sorry, David ... I had no idea he would be so ...'

When he got in from work, having fed Sid his Spratt's Dry Cat Food, and opened the door of the flat, Dicky had found David sitting at the kitchen table clutching a box of Kleenex tissues in one hand and a copy of 'The Critical Review' in the other.

'This is the end!' wailed David. 'When the finance people see this it will give them the ammunition they need to shut the show!'

'Oh, I'm sure it won't come to that, although he was

quite … quite …'

'Acerbic? Vicious? Cutting?'

'Outspoken, or direct. I did think he could have been kinder to such a well loved old show. It is quite an institution, after all.'

'He thinks the right institution for it is an old people's home. Look, he says as much here!'

'Have you heard anything from any of the other cast members?'

'Oh, only about absolutely all of them. Don't touch the telephone, it is probably still red hot … What am I going to *do?* When my father sees that, and he will, he will be on at me about getting a proper job, or banging on about starting at the bottom of his business again …'

'I'm sure it won't be that bad …'

'Oh, but it might. I do not want to *run* theatres. I want to act in them!'

-oOo-

Chapter 27

Big plans

'So,' said Annie, 'when we have the opening 'do' will you and The Heartaches, come and play, Heather?'

'And I suppose ye want me to get other acts tae come along too?' said Heather, scowling into the telephone. 'And given what you told us about Hamish, you will expect them to do it for nowt, ahm guessing.'

'Och, no, Heather. You don't understand. Uncle Jock and I are in charge of the entertainments side of the business. You will be properly paid at the going rate.'

'Did you just say "the business," Annie?'

'Aye. We have formed a Company and … and I'm a Director!'

-oOo-

'It's for you,' said David, placing the handset on the table in the hall.

'Dicky, it's me, Milly,' said Camilla.

A surge of pure excitement ripped along Dicky's spine.

'Ah, yes. Hello. Um. How are things?' he blustered.

'And nice to speak to you too, I'm sure!' said Camilla, chuckling to herself at Dicky's awkwardness. She found his shyness attractive, but couldn't resist occasionally teasing.

'We have a bit of a problem,' she said. 'But I've thought up a solution which might work. What is your middle name?'

'Pardon?'

'Your middle name, Dicky. I assume you have one?'

'I, er, yes. It's James.'

'James. That is a nice name, I like that. Well, you might have to use it as a "pen name" when you are introduced to Uncle Herb ...'

'I'm sorry, I don't think I follow ...'

'No, of course you don't, you poor sap. You haven't a clue what I'm talking about yet have you? Well, listen ...'

-oOo-

'I'm no sure,' said Hamish.

'Well, the idea is a great improvement on tents,' said Uncle Jock.

'Aye, and we'll be able tae move them and mow underneath,' said Annie.

Hamish sighed. He knew when he was beaten.

'Well ah think we should go down tae London again to look at them first, don't you?'

'Aye,' said Uncle Jock.

'Will I ring up Milly and see if we can stay again?' asked Annie, and seeing the look of uncertainty in Hamish's eye, she added, 'Then you can see Dicky, and get on the beer w'him.'

It was enough. Hamish agreed that Annie could telephone Camilla, and if they could stay again some-time next week, he would tell John that he would be over to look at his second-hand touring caravans.

-oOo-

'I see what you mean,' said Dame Amelia. 'Quite a comprehensive critique of the premise on which the play is based.'

Herb had calmed down a little after the initial shock,

but was still wounded by Dicky's review.

'Yes, but ... Well, I suppose it is no good ducking the issue. Between ourselves, Amelia, I rather got talked into this one on the basis that the Wimbledon Theatre became available and could be secured at very advantageous rates ...'

'And you didn't do quite as much background digging into the play itself as you otherwise might have done?'

'I can never get anything past you, can I Amelia. All right, I admit it, I made a mistake, and perhaps the play is not as good as I initially thought it was. But this guy in 'The Critical Review' has spotted every wrinkle in the damn thing, and pointed out flaws in it that I had no idea were there. I'll have to take it off, of course.'

'Did you sell many seats?'

'No. And there were more than average returns ...'

'When you say returns?'

'Oh, all right. People demanding their money back. There is always a bit of that, usually towards the last curtain of any new show, when folk try it on, to get to see it for nothing. But this time, yes, I have to admit, there have been complaints.'

'Could you not let it run for a while to see if this review has any effect on the box office?'

'I think the days are gone when getting a play panned by the critics more or less guaranteed its success. Audiences these days tend to trust reviewers a bit more, and reviewers have got much better at gauging the public mood.'

'Well, you would know all about that, of course, Herb. But where does that leave the theatre in Wimbledon?'

'Well, how do I know?'

'Herb, think about it. If you let this show rub along for a few weeks and then can it, you will still have the lease on the theatre.'

'So?'

'So, how long do you think it will take to set up this play from the new chap we have been talking about? If it can be done quickly enough, the theatre need not be dark for long, or anytime at all, and you can open with a whole new show, which I think you already know is pretty hot stuff.'

'It needs a bit of work, Amelia. I told you that.'

'Well, the sooner we start …'

'Yes, I see your point. You make a convincing argument, Amelia. You always did. I wish you would consider …'

'Herb! We have talked about this …'

'I know, I know. But Amelia I have been so lonely …'

'Ah! There is the gong for lunch. Come along, Herb. Mrs Childs has surpassed herself with the most exquisite cold game pie, I can't wait to see what you think of it.'

-oOo-

'So, what I thought was,' said Camilla, 'if I introduced you as Dicky James, Uncle Herb might not make the connection to 'The Critical Review' and your critique of his new play 'Not Real Soldiers'.

Dicky felt he was losing his grip on the lucky streak that had served him so well lately.

'Uncle Herb?'

'Well, he is not my real uncle, of course, but I started calling him that when I was little, and it sort of stuck. He is Sir Herbert Walters, the promoter behind that play.'

'And,' said Dicky, now catching on quickly, 'is the person Dame Amelia wanted to introduce me to, and talk about *my* play this weekend …'

'Got it in one. Smart boy!' said Camilla.

'Oh, no …'

'Well, come on. Cheer up Dicky. If he thinks you are Dicky James he might not make the connection with the review written under the name Richard Bourne.'

'Yes, he will. My name, Richard Bourne, I mean, appears top right on each page of the manuscript I gave to your mother.'

'Ah,' said Camilla. 'That puts rather a different complexion on it.'

-oOo-

Chapter 28

Fancy footwork

'So ahm ringing you up because Annie got noo reply when she telephoned to Camilla's flat, Dicky.'

'She is down at her mother's house, Hamish. Getting ready for this weekend house party tomorrow, where I expect to be torn limb from limb.'

'Wha' ever are ye maithering about, Dicky. Why should ye be torn limb from limb? We, that is Annie and I, want tae come doon again and buy some caravans, and ah thought we could get a beer or two …'

'Caravans?' asked Dicky.

-oOo-

'So, I'm sorry to call you to the telephone again …'

'I'm not. I'm pleased you rang me.'

'Well, it is just that Hamish called and asked ...'

'Oh, so you didn't just ring because you were missing me, and wanted to hear my voice?' said Camilla.

'Erm ...'

'It's all right Dicky, I'm just teasing ... you were saying Hamish was on the telephone?'

'Yes, and he wants to know if you would mind if he and Annie stayed with you next Tuesday and Wednesday night, while they buy some caravans ...'

'Caravans?'

'It's a long story.'

'Yes, of course they can come, and you can tell me all about it tomorrow, when you come down to Holme Hall, and we try to sort out this play thing.'

'I've made a mess of that, haven't I,' said Dicky.

'Not necessarily. I went and poured my heart out to Mummy about it earlier, and she said to leave it to her. Uncle Herb would do anything for her, you see. At one point I thought he and Mummy ...'

'Even with the best will in the world, I can't see how I can make this right. I guess my hopes for the play are doomed.'

'Don't be too sure, chum. My mother and I may have had our moments, but I do admire her ability to find a way through the scaliest of scrapes. She is pure charm, you know, when she wants to be.'

'I can well imagine that. She has the most amazing voice, you know ...'

'And with a little help from her friends at Paramount Pictures, it made her fortune ...'

'You know sometimes your voice is very similar, such as when you ... when you ...'

'When I?'

'Erm ... when you held my hand the other night after our date and asked me to feed Sid.'

Camilla laughed, and that broke the spell. Abashed, Dicky couldn't think of anything else to say.

'That reminds me. You are keeping an eye on Sid, and doing his food as I asked, aren't you?'

'Yes, he is fine. I'll tell Hamish what you said ... and ... and ... can I just say that ... well ... that I would really like to be able to call you up just to tell you I was missing you, and how much I wanted to hear your voice ...'

'Well, you can listen to my voice for real tomorrow. Sleep tight now, and in between thinking of me, keep thinking of how we can help mummy sweeten Uncle Herb up. Does he know you are living in one of his flats, by the way?'

'Pardon?'

'I said ...'

'I heard! Does Uncle Herb, I mean Sir Herbert Walters, own my, I mean David's flat?'

'Yes, and mine. David is his step-son. I thought you knew ...'

'But I thought his name was David Leslie?'

'It is. Leslie was his father's name and he uses it professionally so he does not appear to gain any advantage from Herb's illustrious history.'

'Oh, Lordy! He's going to sling me out of David's flat too, when he finds out I'm living there, isn't he ...'

-oOo-

After raising Hamish on the telephone, delivering Camilla's message and preparing himself a light supper, Dicky took himself off to bed.

He did not expect to be able to sleep well, and he was proved correct.

The morning found him in an uncomfortable tangle of bed sheets. He had spent the night tossing and turning, during which he was alternately either too hot or too cold.

After a bath and a boiled egg he did feel a little better, but even the prospect of seeing Camilla again did not assuage his feeling of impending doom. His prospects, he thought, were grim, as he packed his case and prepared to drive to Surrey.

'Rather you than me,' said David, leaning on the door frame as Dicky closed his case.

'I'm sorry?'

'Going to deliberately hob-nob with Sir Herbert Walters, after what you put in that review.'

'Camilla has told me he is your step-father, David.'

'Yes, I'm sorry about that. If I had known you were going to review one of his productions I could have put you wise, but I confess I have never even heard of this 'Not Real Soldiers' thing.'

'Nothing to apologise for, old man. My problem entirely. And as you said, it is my job after all, nothing personal. I'm only sorry that my stay here has been so short. I hope you will find another sharer quickly.'

'Do you think he will cast you out into the snow?'

'Probably, I'm just grateful it is August and quite warm.'

'That is probably why I can't draw an appropriate Shakespearian quotation to mind to match the occasion.'

'No gallows humour then?'

'Well, it is not Shakespeare, but would this do? ... "Build a man a fire and he'll be warm for the night. Set a man on fire and he'll be warm for the rest of his life." Will that suffice until I come up with something more appropriate?'

Dicky laughed and began to feel a little better.

'Ah, a laugh at last from the boy! "Then I'll play the happy fool and get laugh lines on my face. I'd rather overload my liver with wine than starve my heart by denying myself fun." - The Merchant of Venice.'

-o0o-

'Thank you, Amelia. Our little chat has helped me to see things in a new light,' said Sir Herbert Walters, helping himself to another sausage from the sideboard, where the breakfast had been laid out, and coating it liberally in tomato ketchup.

'I'm glad you see it my way, Herb,' smiled Dame Amelia, squeezing his arm gently. 'It will be so good to see the young people happy, and you might find it all works out splendidly.'

'I hope you are right. It is quite a financial risk ...'

'Oh I'm sure that once you roll your sleeves up and smack into it, the old Herb Walters genius will ride to the rescue and save the day, just as it always has in the past. The way you work at things and encourage people to give of their best has always been one of the qualities I admire most about you, Herb.'

-oOo-

Chapter 29

Confrontation

Harry Jarvis was trying to keep a low profile, and so far, as only a couple of the guests had arrived and his duties amounted simply to parking their cars, he had been successful.

There was no sign of the little black Austin A30 with that silly psychedelic flower painted on the boot, and Harry intended to bolt into his flat, above the motor-house, and stay there, as soon as it appeared.

He rubbed his arm as the memory of his last encounter with its owners came back to him.

-oOo-

There was something wrong.

'Come on, Petal, what's the matter?'

As he tried to coax the car along, it was making

rattling noises and seemed to be rapidly losing power. Each encouraging dab of the accelerator seemed only to produce a small cloud of blue smoke and a cough, but no corresponding increase in speed.

The car was still going, at least, but progress was becoming increasingly slow and tortuous, and Dicky wondered if they were about to break down.

'You can do it, Petal,' said Dicky. 'Not that far now, and I can take you to that nice little workshop by the station in Woodlesham, where we bought petrol. I'm sure they can sort you out. Just please get me to Holme Hall, first.'

-oOo-

'You rang, ma'am?'

'Yes, Simpkin. When Mr Richard Bourne arrives, will you show him straight up to my private study before he meets the other guests, and inform me that he has arrived.'

'Very good, ma'am.'

Nobody, thought Simpkin, ever gets shown into her private rooms. What's all this about?

'And then find Camilla and tell her to join us there ...'

Simpkin was intrigued and resolved to position himself nearby when this meeting started, to ensure he could hear what was being said.

Returning to the kitchens, he explained what he had been told to Mrs Childs and sought her views on the matter.

'Seems clear enough to me, Rufus,' said the cook, sliding a tray of scones into the oven. 'Since she was given her freedom with that flat in London, perhaps she has been being a little too free with this young gentleman of hers ...'

'You are not suggesting ...'

'My money is on wedding bells inside a month, and a new baby in the nursery not long after.'

'Mrs Childs!' said Simpkin, 'Surely not! Not my little Milly ... Why, she is barely more than a child. This will break Dame Amelia's heart!'

-oOo-

The little Austin puffed and popped its way along the drive as Holme Hall came into view at last, but then, just as they reached the roundabout affair by the front door, the engine wheezed and stopped in a cloud of smoke, with a final rattle.

'Well done, Petal,' said Dicky under his breath as Simpkin, the butler, approached and none too gently wrenched open the door.

'Good evening, Mr Bourne. If you would like to accompany me, your luggage will be attended too and this ...ah ... motor car ... will be parked for you.'

-oOo-

Dame Amelia was already waiting in her private study on the first floor. Dicky had only just sat down in the seat she offered when Camilla entered, and he had to spring up again.

'Thank you for coming,' Dame Amelia was saying. 'Now, I see no point in dragging this out, so if you don't mind, I should like to deal with the ... the awkward situation which has arisen straight away.'

Here it comes, thought Dicky. She is going to throw me straight out again, as soon as she has told me she is not interested in the play, and delivered Uncle Herb's ultimatum to move out of the flat.

'Mummy was so impressed with your play, Dicky. We all were ...' said Camilla, fixing a smile.

'It certainly has potential,' purred Dame Amelia. 'In a little while I shall introduce you to Sir Herbert Walters, the impresario, who has also read it. But there is, as you will have established by now, a certain matter to be a addressed in relation to your critique of 'Not Real Soldiers', in which Herb, ah, Sir Herbert, heads a consortium of financiers backing the play. As you might expect he was a little disappointed by that.'

'I'm sorry, Dame Amelia. When I wrote that review I had no idea that Sir Herbert ...'

'And would it have made any difference if you did know? I hope not. And Camilla has assured me that you are a man of integrity, and that you write honest reviews without kowtowing to any external pressures.'

'I try to write as I see it. I am sorry if ...'

'But that is all behind us now, isn't it, Mummy? Uncle Herb admits the show is a lemon and is actually quite grateful to Dicky for pointing out some flaws in it he had missed ...'

'Thank you, Camilla. I was coming to that.'

'Sorry, Mummy,' said Camilla subsiding into her chair.

'The thing we must address,' said Dame Amelia, as Dicky heard the starter motor of the little Austin churn outside, 'is how to take matters forward.'

As they heard the car, on the drive below them, popping and shuddering reluctantly into life, and then, with a dispiriting rattle, stalling, at the hands of persons unknown, Dicky looked down at his shoes.

'You are a most charming young man, Richard, ah, Dicky, and my daughter has explained to me, at some length, that her feelings for you go beyond just friendship. I have to tell you ... please don't interrupt, that nothing; nothing at all, matters more to me than my daughter's happiness, so I have taken it upon myself to speak to Sir Herbert to, shall we say, plead your case.'

'I ... I ...' stuttered Dicky.

'Oh, Mummy ...' said Camilla.

'I am not without influence, even today, in the circles in which Herb, ah, Sir Herbert moves, and I hope you will find that, perhaps with a little humility on your part when you meet, the unfortunate matter of the review can be laid to rest. But let me say this, Rich ... ah, Dicky, if you are paltering with my daughter's affections in the hope of any sort of financial gain, I will withdraw my support immediately, and will not allow Camilla to speak to you again.'

'Dame Amelia, I assure you ...' began Dicky.

'Oh, Mummy!' said Camilla rising from her chair and rushing to embrace her mother. 'You really are a wonder. If Uncle Herb will still back the play and let Dicky stay living in David's flat, I'm sure this is going to be brilliant. Just Brilliant. Dicky is so clever and ... well, you have seen how good the play is ... and I ... and I ...'

'Yes, thank you, Camilla. Do you feel ready to meet Sir Herbert and my other guests, Dicky?' smiled Dame Amelia.

Dicky was in a daze as they left the private study

in single file, and was only dimly aware of the retreating back of Simpkin, the butler, ahead of them at the foot of the stairs.

With the words 'her feelings for you go beyond just friendship' ringing in his ears, as he tried to concentrate on walking, rather than dancing, down the steps, Dicky heard the little Austin's starter motor grind once more, and then with a throaty roar, the engine sprang into life.

'Is there something wrong with your car, Dicky?' asked Camilla.

'I shall ask Jarvis to have a look at it for you,' said Dame Amelia.

-oOo-

Sir Herbert was in the yellow drawing room, Simpkin had informed them, and he opened the doors to the opulently decorated room with a respectful bow.

Sir Herbert Walters was a tall upright man with a fine head of black hair and a neatly trimmed moustache under a prominent nose. He shook hands firmly with Dicky as he was introduced, and opened the proceedings.

'First of all, can I mention that while I was a little taken aback when I first read it, young man, I have to say that, on reflection, your review of 'Not Real Soldiers' made some sense to me,' Sir Herbert's soft

American accent betrayed only a little annoyance. 'Although it is supposed to be a lighthearted play, there are some factual inaccuracies that may jar with those who recently went through National Service, such as yourself, and those boys in the Regular Army serving at the time. For that, let me apologise ...'

'It is I who should apologise ...' said Dicky.

'What for?' said Camilla. 'If a show is no good, it is no good, and there is no point in false praise.'

'I wouldn't go so far as to say it was no good. It did have some funny moments and some of the characters were well drawn, I thought ...' said Dicky, beginning to relax.

'Shall we draw a line under this and move to discussing Dicky's own play,' said Dame Amelia.

'Fair enough,' said Sir Herbert. 'Now your play has definite promise, young man, although there are quite a few things which do need attention ...'

'I loved it, Dicky,' said Camilla moving closer and slipping her arm through his.

'Well, I'm more than ready to learn, Sir Herbert. It is my first effort and I'm sure it would really benefit from anything you may have noticed. And thank you very much for taking the time to read it through, by the way.'

'We made a list of points to go through, Dicky,' said Dame Amelia. 'If we can tidy those up, I can tell you that Herb and I are prepared to head up a consortium of investors to look at the possibility of staging the play.'

'Crikey!' said Dicky. 'I mean thank you. Thank you very much!'

'I'm afraid some of the comments we have to make are quite direct, Dicky,' Sir Herbert said, running a hand through his hair. 'They are not meant to offend, but are the things we would need you to be prepared to rewrite or alter, if we were to back you.'

'Of course, yes. I understand,' said Dicky, swallowing hard and wondering what was coming next.

'Would you like to go through the list now?' asked Dame Amelia, as Camilla tightened her grip on his arm.

'Yes, yes please. If you can spare the time …'

'Well,' said Sir Herbert, clearing his throat. 'Some of the dialogue is a bit baggy, but the first thing that will have to be changed is the title … "The Sunken Treasure From Port Aloo" sounds like something valuable dropped down a chemical toilet …'

-oOo-

'And she sent me out to the Post Office to get them to Roneo copy this play, so she could hand out copies to some of the guests what's coming. That's what it's all about, Mrs Childs, just that!'

'So young Camilla is not expecting?'

'Certainly not. And I'll thank you not to cast such aspersions on your employer's good name.'

'Pity,' said Mrs Childs. 'It would have been nice to have a baby in the house. So do you know what this play all about then, Rufus?'

'Well, as it happened, the Postmistress wanted me to check the first Roneo copy before she made any more, The machine is new, you see, and she is still familiarising herself with it, and I took the opportunity to run an eye over it.'

'When did you do that?'

'On my half day. I took the manuscript in for copying and went to sit outside the Horse and Groom with the first copy to come off the machine …'

'And a pint or two of 'Old Docker', no doubt.'

'Well, it was my half day …'

'So what is it all about? Is it a romance?'

'Nah, I didn't read it all, of course, but it seems to be about some young toff who finds out about a boat what's sunk off Cornwall, full of valuable items someone pinched from an Indian prince in a place called Aloo, or something like that. The toff is trying to get up a group to go and get the treasure from the wreck.'

'So not a romance then?'

'Not as I could see. Bit boring, I thought.'

-o0o-

'So, Jarvis, while Mr Bourne is here, would you examine his little car, please, and tell us what is wrong with it.'

Harry was mortified. This would almost certainly mean he would have to talk to Dicky Bourne, and he wanted to avoid doing that more than anything.

'Jarvis here was training to be a motor mechanic whilst in the RAF, ma'am,' said Simpkin with a sly sideways glance at the quaking chauffeur. 'He assured us that there is very little to do with the ailments of motor cars that he cannot repair, and that statement, and his experience, helped us to select him for the job as your chauffeur, if you recall, Dame Amelia.'

'I confess I had forgotten that detail,' said Dame Amelia. 'But in that case, would you please carry out whatever repairs are necessary, Jarvis, and ensure the car is ready and running properly by the end of the weekend for Mr Bourne to return home in it.'

'But, beggin' your pardon, ma'am, what about parts and whatnot, the workshop is equipped to service a

Bentley, not that ... not that old car.'

'I'm sure Dame Amelia will allow you to order what you need from the workshop in Woodlesham, by the railway station ...'

'Yes, of course, Simpkin. Will you ensure they submit an account for whatever is needed.'

'Certainly, ma'am. May I excuse Jarvis now, to make a start on the work?'

-oOo-

Chapter 30

Appeasement

Still clutching the list of 'Points to go through' that Dame Amelia had referred to, Dicky was introduced to more of the guests as they arrived.

First there was Marsha and Ira Samuels, she a retired actress, he a city financier with property all over London.

Then there was Sir Philip and Lady Marchmont-Bone. Familiar names, of course, from the world of literature and publishing.

Then, with a sharp cough, Simpkin announced the arrival of Darren Beamish the Australian film producer, and a Miss Alice Peabody, who was noticeable principally for her very short mini-dress.

Next Dame Hermione Bishop, accompanied by Arthur Milsop, playwright, and their son Samuel

Milsop-Bishop.

The list seemed to go on and on and Dicky thought he would never remember all their names, as one by one, or rather in couples, Dame Amelia started to introduce him to them.

Other than pleasantries, the only one of the guests who actually stated an opinion about the play at this point was Darren Beamish, who said he liked the play but thought some of the dialogue was too flaccid, which caused Miss Peabody, clutching his arm perhaps to avoid an awkward fall from her stiletto heels, to giggle.

-oOo-

Hamish had been concerned about his visit to see the Planning Officer at the local council offices, but he was surprised at how welcoming they were to the idea of setting up the campsite and facilities in the castle grounds.

'He said if it bought employment and tourism tae the area they would welcome it, Uncle Jock. I could nae be more pleased!'

'That's the last wee hurdle,' smiled Annie. 'You had better find a builder to put in those loos.'

'Aye, and a caterer for all them dinners.'

-oOo-

The cough Simpkin gave in his immediate rear

surprised Harry and he banged his head for the third time on the open bonnet of the Austin A30.

'Nasty little car,' he muttered under his breath. 'What do you want?'

'Have you found the problem yet, young Harry?'

'No, I ain't. What d'you want to offer to get it fixed for anyway. It's only fit for the scrap heap!'

'You said you could fix motors. I made a note of that during your job interview. But of course, if that wasn't true, we shall have to see about that.'

'Waddayer mean?' asked Harry, wiping his hands on a rag.

'Lying in a job interview is grounds, you know.'

'Grounds? What are you talking about?'

'Grounds for dismissal. I'm not saying Dame Amelia would 'ave you out on your ear, but I distinctly heard her telling the other guests how fond she was of this Dicky bloke and how she would do what she could to help 'im.'

'What's that got ta do with me?'

'Well, she is not going to be best pleased if her chauffeur is not a man of his word and can't mend this car when she's specifically offered, in good faith, is she.'

'Now wait a minute ...'

'No, you wait a minute, young Harry. I'm prepared to turn a blind eye to your inadequacies on this occasion if you run the little car up to the workshop by the station and get them to tell you what is wrong. Of course if you can fix it then, so be it, but if you can't, you will have to get them to do it.'

'I think the engine has blown a gasket or something like that.'

'And Dame Amelia will likely blow a gasket if you don't get it fixed by the time the guests start going home.'

'But I,'

'And then young Mr Bourne may become agitated, and you have already explained that he has verlent tendencies. I heard 'im telling Miss Camilla he was perticlar fond of that little motor. Who knows what he will do to you if he finds out you are not really a mechanic. He might jump to the conclusion that you 'ad made it worse.'

'He wouldn't ... would he?'

'Best you get the little car up to the workshop before they close for the night, young Harry.'

-oOo-

The four piece ensemble Dame Amelia had hired to provide music for the evening was setting up in one corner of the large dining room, when Mrs Childs swept in to check on the arrangements.

'I hope you can play something with a bit of swing to it,' she observed having introduced herself to their leader. 'Dame Amelia and Sir Herb Walters like to cut a rug, you know.'

-oOo-

While her guests enjoyed a cocktail and renewed old acquaintances, Dame Amelia and Sir Herbert Walters invited Dicky to join them in the library for the first of several discussions about the play.

Despite the warm and humid evening, there were still the embers of a fire glowing in the grate although, in due deference to her guests' preferences, it was the only one still lit in the house.

When they reached the library, Dicky found that Sir Philip and Lady Marchmont-Bone were already there and clutching a copy of his play, printed in the ubiquitous purple ink which was the typical sign of a Roneo copy.

'Herb,' said Dame Amelia, 'would you explain Phil and Sylvia's interest in this, please.'

'Sure. You see, Dicky, Phil and Sylvia have collaborated with various theatre companies and writers I have been involved with over the years, and I've asked them to come on board with your play, if they are interested.'

'And I have to say we are interested in this, young man,' said Sir Philip. 'Although as Herb has no doubt told you, there are several things we will need …'

'Yes, well, would you mind if I left you to discuss the finer points?' asked Dame Amelia. 'With a house full of guests …'

'Of course, of course,' chimed Sir Philip and Lady Marchmont-Bone, in unison.

-oOo-

The cast meeting had not gone well and David was not the only one who expressed the view that the 'writing was on the wall', in the pub afterwards.

'How long do you think we have got?' asked a startled-looking lighting engineer.

'Anybody's guess,' boomed a seasoned actor in a robust baritone.

'The accountants men said something about decisions being made in September,' stated a handsome young man, running a hand through his thick hair.

'Well, that's it. We will be off by October,' added a tall thin actress with a sneer. 'I knew it.'

-oOo-

'So I hoped, Arthur, that you would be prepared to edit the manuscript and work with Dicky to tighten it up here and there.'

Dame Amelia had invited Arthur Milsop to join them in the Library and now handed him over to Sir Herbert Walters to discuss the details.

'Very interesting,' Arthur was saying. 'I shall enjoy working on this with you, Dicky, if you will allow me …'

'Oh, rather! I mean yes, please, if you can spare the time,' said Dicky. 'I've read two of your plays, and some years ago my parents took me to see …'

'Ah, I do hope you will excuse me again,' interrupted Dame Amelia. 'Can I leave you for a moment … Oh, and Dicky, I think Camilla is planning on playing tennis in the morning with Arthur's son, Sammy. I've heard he is rather good, if you fancied a game tomorrow. Now, I must get back to my guests …'

-oOo-

Darren Beamish was showing off to the leggy Alice Peabody, and boasting to Marsha and Ira Samuels, that he had enough money to fund Dickie's play on his own.

'I'm sure you have,' said Marsha. 'I heard you did very well in some property deal, so Ira was telling me. He is always interested in property deals.'

'Very nice,' said Ira Samuels, who was openly ogling Alice Peabody.

'The property deal, dear?'

'Er, yes,' said Ira realising that he had let his attention wander and been caught doing it.

As they moved away to talk to some of the other guests, Marsha took her husband none too gently by the arm.

'Stop making appointments your body can't keep, you old fool. She is young enough to be that revolting Australian's daughter, and you are easily old enough to be her grandfather!'

-oOo-

Chapter 31

Mostly about food

To avoid the attentions of Sammy Milsop-Bishop, Camilla had attached herself to Simpkin, the butler, and was overseeing the distribution of drinks and canapés.

Phil and Sylvia had been for a walk around the gardens, after their initial meeting with Dicky, and returning now, Sylvia caught her eye.

'He seems very nice,' she said with a slow stage wink.

'Do you know him well, Lady Marchmont-Bone,' asked Camilla.

'No, we have only just met.'

'Then can I speak candidly to you about him?'

'I suppose so dear, if you like ...'

'He is somewhat dim, if you ask me, and rather adhesive. I would rather he left me alone.'

Lady Marchmont-Bone took a sharp intake of breath. 'But I thought... Well, what with all this talk of the play and whatnot, I naturally assumed you two were an item!'

'I'm sorry, to disappoint you Lady Marchmont-Bone, but I regard Sammy Milsop-Bishop as a bit tedious.'

'Oh, so do we!' said Sir Philip, chortling. 'But I think Sylvia may have been talking about young Dicky Bourne!'

-oOo-

As the dinner gong sounded, Dicky, released from the latest discussions on the finer points of his play in the library, went in search of Camilla.

On the way he found Simpkin, returning from his duties with the gong and on his way to the kitchen.

'Which way is the dining room, please,' he asked.

'At the bottom of the stairs on the left, sir. You will see the double doors straight ahead of you when you return from putting on your lounge suit and tie.'

Simpkin let a little smile play about the corners of his mouth as Dicky thanked him, said he had forgotten about that, and dashed up to his room.

-oOo-

Alice Peabody was wearing a long, slim, pale-yellow dress with a plunging neckline and a concoction of pearls and no-doubt expensive jewellery.

She smiled winningly at Simpkin, as he opened the dining room doors.

'Can I get a whiskey sour in 'ere?' she asked, as Darren Beamish propelled her towards the table.

'I think three is enough, don't you?' he said. 'And don't forget there will be wine with the grub.'

'Orright, Darren, darlin', don't fuss. I am gettin' a bit tipsy, as it 'appens. They mix 'em strong 'ere!'

As they took their seats, Alice picked up the menu card from the middle of the table and studied it.

'Blimey, Darren, it's all in foreign. How the hell d'ya know what you're eating?'

'Cripes, you're right, but some of it is in English underneath ... Let's have a look at that'

He read ...

Entrée : asperges rôties au four
(Oven-roasted asparagus)

Potage :
(Soup : Escoffier's Oxtail Soup)

Poisson :
(Fish : Smoked trout)

Plat : un carré d'agneau en croûte d'herbes
(Half oven, half pan lamb, with herbs, etc.)

Accompagnement : gratin dauphinois, etc.
(Potatoes, cream, butter, garlic, etc.)

Sorbet :

Dessert : tarte au citron etc.
(Sweet and sour lemon tart, fresh fruit and nuts)

Fromage :
(Cheese selection)

Cafe, petits fours, etc :

As Darren puzzled over the menu, Simpkin arrived at Alice's elbow.

'Sparkling Crémant d'Alsace or Hock, miss?' he enquired.

'Wass 'ee say?' asked Alice.

-oOo-

Returning in his lounge suit and tie, Dicky found Camilla standing at the bottom of the staircase.

He could not help gasping when she moved into a better-lit area of the hall. Her elegant, full-length silver dress subtly emphasised her shapeliness and the light make-up she had applied accentuated her features superbly.

'My goodness, Camilla. You are beautiful!' said Dicky

before he could stop himself.

'Yes, well. I thought you were never coming and all this would have been for nothing …'

'I'm sorry, I had to change …'

'If you had taken much longer, I would have had to go into dinner with that clingy creep Sammy Milsop-Bishop!'

-oOo-

'Well, that was quite splendid,' said Lady Marchmont-Bone at the conclusion of the meal.

'Thank you, dear,' said Dame Amelia. 'I'm glad you enjoyed it. Perhaps we girls can slip off to the drawing room, where I believe coffee and petits fours will be served, and we can leave the chaps to their Port.'

'Right-ho,' said Marsha Samuels, rising from the table. 'Now, remember what I said, Ira, just one glass.'

At the other end of the table Darren nudged Alice who had been staring vacantly into the middle distance for quite a while.

'I think I'd better go to bed,' she whispered. 'I'm pooped.'

Meanwhile, Dicky dragged his eyes away from Camilla as she drifted out of the room with her mother, and turned his attention to Sammy Milsop-Bishop, who was saying something about Port.

'Port, eh? Yes, Port. Jolly good. Rather!' and catching Simpkin's eye, 'Yes, please, my dear old butler, what!'

-oOo-

'So, what I think is that to increase the audience penetration and build up public awareness, we should produce a version of it which can be serialised and broadcast on the British radio.'

Darren sat back in his chair and allowed his glass to be refilled.

'That will fill the theatre with people eager to see the play,' he added.

'But won't that give the plot away, and have the opposite effect, and keep people away from the live performance?' asked Sir Herbert Walters.

'Depends on the timing,' said Darren, waving his glass confidently. 'If it is launched as a play first, then a little while later, after the initial interest has died down a bit, put on the radio ...'

'I see what you mean,' said Arthur Milsop. 'I confess I have not heard of doing that before, but it is an idea.'

Dicky watched in bemusement as all this went on. It was hard to comprehend that all these rich and, in some cases, famous people were talking about his play.

'I'm afraid I have never written a serialisation,' he said.

'No, but I have,' said Arthur Milsop. 'If we all think it's a good idea, I could take that on, for a modest fee, of course.'

'Be that as it may,' said Ira Samuels, allowing Simpkin to fill his glass for the third time. 'What this project needs, indeed what anything new coming to the market needs, is a good, solid, advertising budget and a carefully-thought-out marketing plan, kicking in some time before it opens. If people don't know the play is coming, nobody is going to buy tickets.'

'Good point, Ira,' said Herb. 'Of course that is going to take a bit of, what shall we call it … 'seed-corn investment' up front, from those of us who are interested in this. By the way, should we have a show of hands just to be clear who is interested in investing in this?'

Dicky held his breath. Everyone raised a hand except Arthur and Sammy Milsop-Bishop.

'Arthur?' enquired Herb.

'Well, my role will be to take money out, for work on the play and this radio script, if we go down that road; rather than put any in as I see it …' said Arthur, looking slightly sheepish.

'And no point looking at me,' added his son. 'The cupboard is bare, I'm afraid. All I've got to my name is not quite enough to cover a few outstanding tailor's bills.'

'I can get my lawyers to draw up a sort of partnership agreement on Monday and send it round to you all, if you agree.' said Herb. 'They are familiar with this sort of arrangement, of course, and I'm sure they can quickly iron out the details.'

'Percentages, you mean?' said Darren. 'Risk and reward calculations, and all that sort of thing.'

'I'm sure that would be part of it, yes,' said Herb. 'So can I assume we are in business, Gentlemen?'

To general assent and nodding, Herb got up from the table and moved round to where Dicky sat.

'Congratulations, Dicky. Your investment team is ready to create the business framework for your first play to be launched!' And he held out his hand for Dicky to shake.

-oOo-

Chapter 32

And relax

In the drawing room, as the gentlemen began to file in, the little four-piece ensemble was playing the sort of easy-listening music heard in some of the better hotel lobbies on either side of the Atlantic.

In readiness for this evening the carpets in one half of the room had been rolled-up and taken away, revealing a polished wooden dance floor.

This room represented slightly over half of the original ballroom, from which it was divided by Dame Amelia's second husband, for when they finally returned from America. He decided, bearing in mind how Dame Amelia felt the cold, that these alterations would create cosier, more liveable spaces, which were easier to heat.

The conversion was only partially successful,

however, principally because of the enormously high ceiling, where the room towered across the entire height of the house. And despite the installation of a positively huge fireplace, it was still difficult to heat, so was now only used for gatherings such as this.

It was nonetheless conveniently positioned just along a broad corridor from the large dining room where they had eaten, and where the musicians played until the ladies withdrew, so it took no time for the ensemble to set up again to be ready for the next stage of the evening.

When the gentlemen entered they took it as a signal to increase the volume and the tempo of the music, and to start the ball rolling, as it were, Sir Herbert asked Dame Amelia for a dance.

As Martha and Ira took to the floor, followed closely by Phil and Sylvia, Dicky moved towards Camilla's chair, but before he could get there, Sammy Milsop-Bishop had offered her a dance and she was rising from her chair, with an apologetic glance over her shoulder for Dicky as she passed by.

'Ahem,' said Dicky, coming to a stop. 'Would you care for this dance, Dame Hermione, if Arthur wouldn't mind, I mean?'

'Arthur? No, he doesn't dance. He is much too clumsy and uncoordinated. I should be delighted ...'

Dame Hermione could certainly dance however, and

Dicky remembered that Camilla had told him she was a 'successful showgirl' before settling down with Arthur and producing the slimy Sammy who was now getting rather too friendly with Camilla for Dicky's liking.

'Don't they make a lovely couple,' said Dame Hermione now. 'And Samuel is a good dancer, don't you think?'

Dicky did not, and as if to confirm his opinion, at that moment Sammy stepped on Camilla's toes.

-oOo-

'How much?' said Rufus Simpkin as Harry helped himself to toast at the table in the kitchen early the next morning.

'Ten quid, they said. The bad running is just a blocked oil filter which they will soak in paraffin overnight then put back in with some new oil,' Harry explained. 'But they spotted that both king-pins was badly worn and could snap at any time. That makes that old banger a danger on the road, that does.'

'And ten pounds will cover both jobs and see the car returned here on Monday morning?'

'That's what they said.'

'Very well, tell them to proceed. If they get it back by ten o'clock, you will probably have ample time to wash and vacuum it, before Mr Bourne wants to leave.'

'Wash and vacuum it!' said Harry incredulously.

'You heard me correctly, young Harry,' smiled the butler. 'And perhaps give it a polish up as well, so I can make a good report on your expertise with cars to Dame Amelia.'

'You wicked old schemer ... I ought to ...'

'Pardon, Harry?'

'Nuffink,' said Harry. 'Nuffink.'

-oOo-

'I thought you were going to dance my feet right off, Dicky,' said Camilla, helping herself to kidneys from the sideboard. 'I'm surprised I am not four inches shorter this morning.'

'Well, I couldn't let the odious Sammy get his wandering hands on you again, now could I? And I did do my duty and danced at least once with all the other ladies.'

'You did. Your stamina was something to behold,' laughed Camilla.

'Are there any more of those kidneys?' asked Dicky. 'I need to build my strength back up to take you to the tennis lawn to watch me beat the ghastly Sammy hollow.'

'Before you do that,' said Sir Herbert Walters, entering the breakfast room, 'Could you spare a few of us time to go through some script notes please, in the library?'

Dicky looked at the copy of the play he had bought with him, positioned beside his place at the breakfast table. It was now much thumbed and covered in hand-written notes on every page, including the blank sides where he had not typed.

'Right-ho,' he said dully.

'Don't worry,' said Camilla. 'I'll soften Sammy up for you. I have a pretty formidable forehand smash you know.'

-oOo-

While Camilla did what she could to exhaust Sammy, and in so doing managed to beat him six games to four, Dicky was working hard and assiduously to knock the script of the play into shape with his new team of backers and supporters.

An entire scene change was declared unnecessary, substantial sections of dialogue were rewritten, and two minor characters were removed from the narrative altogether.

At the end of it, when Sir Herbert asked for a show of hands to confirm that the process was complete to everyone's satisfaction, Dicky, having run out of space to write on the script itself, had seven pages of notes written on both sides of clean white foolscap paper, provided and kept replenished, by Simpkin, the butler.

'Now then,' said Sir Herbert, 'If you will allow me to borrow your notes, I will have one of my typists transpose them and circulate them round to everyone for approval. When that is done, if you wouldn't mind, we will ask you and Arthur here to produce a fair copy which will again be circulated and then typed up as the finished manuscript. Everyone happy with that?'

To relieved general assent on the process proposed, Sir Herbert gathered up Dicky's notes and put them carefully in a brown leather briefcase he had kept at his side throughout the gruelling, morning session.

'I should think,' announced Darren, 'we might say we all deserve a beer at this point, or at the very least a cup of coffee.'

'How right you are,' said Dame Amelia.

In reaction to her almost imperceptible nod, Simpkin withdrew to make arrangements, and Dicky excused himself and went to his room to change into his new tennis shorts.

Some brief but intensive exercise would release his tensions, he thought.

Chapter 33

A bruising experience

'It is all very well you apologising,' said Camilla, 'but look at my poor darling Dicky! I think you have broken his nose, you great clumsy brute. Now keep away from me while I mop up all this blood.'

'It's fine, Camilla, honestly,' said Dicky through the thick towelling cloth she was endeavouring to hold in place on his nose to stem the bleeding.

'It is absolutely *not* all right, sweetheart. I saw him come right up to the net, take aim and swat you with the edge of his racket. He wasn't even attempting to play the ball! Unsportsmanlike at the least, and possibly a deliberate attack.'

'Oh, I say!' said Sammy Milsop-Bishop, 'It was nothing like that, I assure you.'

'Don't give it a second thought, old man,' said Dicky,

wiping blood from his chin with his handkerchief. 'A simple accident. Could have happened to anyone.'

'Does it hurt terribly, my darling?' asked Camilla, as she helped him to his feet, whilst fixing Sammy with a look that could melt glass. 'Let's get you inside and get some cold water on that.'

-oOo-

'Ha, Ha!' chortled Harry. 'I saw it with me own eyes, I did! That Sammy boy caught Dicky-ruddy-Bourne a cracker, right on the hooter! No more 'n he deserves, mind, but there was claret everywhere! Great fun that was! Made my weekend!'

'Oh, dear,' said Mrs Childs, the cook. 'Where did they go? I'll run and see if I can help.'

'Best take the First Aid box, Mrs C.,' said Simpkin. 'There's bandages and all sorts in there.'

-oOo-

After the ministrations of Mrs Childs, and now sporting an enormous bandage across his nose, Dicky sat in a deckchair while Dame Amelia poured him a glass of lemonade and Camilla held his hand.

'So, I'm afraid your car will not be ready until Monday morning. Can you stay until then?' she was saying.

'Well, it is tremendously kind of you to arrange to get it fixed for me, Dame Amelia. You must let me know what it cost …'

'Oh, no, there is no question of that,' purred Dame Amelia. 'These trifling costs are the least we can do. And as I understand it, my driver fixed it himself.'

'But Dicky has got to be back at work on Monday …' said Camilla, tightening her grip on Dicky's hand.

'I could get a train …'

'No, I know. I'll run you back up to town in my two-seater and then we can come back and get your car on Monday evening.'

'Well, that seems a bit of an imposition …'

'Nonsense. Camilla has no other calls on her time at present, so it will give her something useful to do,' said Dame Amelia.

'Just so, Mummy. And anyway I'm not sure Dicky is well enough to drive. He lost an awful lot of blood, you know.'

-oOo-

The little Austin A30 was running better than Dicky could remember. Whatever it was Jarvis had done to it had improved matters no end. It didn't even seem to wander about so much on the road as it used to.

Before they left Holme Hall again on Monday night, having taken the car along the length of the drive and back to try it out, Dicky sought out Harry Jarvis and shook his hand.

'We all square, nah, Mr Bourne?' he had asked.

'Certainly!' said Dicky, and the relief on the chauffeur's face was tangible.

-oOo-

Chapter 34

Planning for the future

Herb Walters was first and foremost a businessman.

To consider his options fully, he took himself off quietly and alone to the Wimbledon Theatre to watch a performance of 'Not Real Soldiers'. He was wondering if Dicky Bourne's review really was the last nail in the coffin for the show.

The auditorium was only about a third full when he purchased his ticket at the door from an attendant who did not recognise him. He took a seat near the back and stayed for about three quarters of the performance. Camilla had described bad plays as 'lemons', and he found her term fitted what he had seen perfectly. It was dire, and would have to come off.

Armed with that first-hand information, Herb resolved to re-double his efforts to get 'Sunken Treasure' ready for the stage as soon as could be managed. His focus now became ensuring that the theatre remained 'dark' with no production playing for the shortest amount of time possible, to keep his losses to a minimum.

-oOo-

Dicky had to temper his excitement when he got back to the flat, where he found David in no mood to celebrate.

The cast was on notice that the number of remaining performances of 'My Fair Lady' was being calculated by the faceless bean-counters now in charge of its future, and David was in a black mood.

'It would be better if it happened at any other time of year,' he complained. 'But shows are closing all over the place, and the Christmas shows have already appointed their casts and are in preparation. There is nothing.'

'Nothing?' asked Dicky.

'Well, I've begged a look at a couple of scripts for things coming up, but you see, at the bottom of the profession where I sit, ordinary jobbing roles are fought over like meat in a tiger's cage. Even my agent is talking about going off to Brighton or somewhere equally ghastly for a holiday, while things are so quiet.'

-oOo-

Economies would have to be made. The losses from 'Not Real Soldiers' could not be entirely off-set, and whilst the Wimbledon theatre may not be as expensive to operate as one in the West End, costs would soon be mounting up.

Herb considered which of the existing cast could be re-deployed to roles in the new play, and if the weasel words in the contracts could force them to join the new company at the same, or even reduced rates, following the failure of their show. He disliked bullying people, but he had to face facts.

The likes of lighting engineers, scene shifters and so on could easily be offered continued employment, but fresh scenery would have to be made, programmes would have to be printed, advertising would have to be paid for, and all the myriad of costs involved in putting on a new show would have to be covered. And it seemed to Herb that little of the paraphernalia he had already paid for to be used in 'Not Real Soldiers' could be given a new lease of life in 'Sunken Treasure'.

None, he decided, of the more recognised actors in the old production were suitable for roles in the new show, or even worth retaining, and even some of the younger members of the cast did not seem so vibrant now as they did during the auditions. The lack-lustre show had knocked all the fight out of them, and he doubted if any could be retained.

Perhaps, he thought, he should follow Dame Amelia's suggestion and give some 'unknowns' a chance with 'Sunken Treasure'. He could always throw them out and replace them if they didn't work out, without the upheaval and potential for bad press if some of the bigger names were dismissed from the show.

The budget would have to be kept tight if the new show was to make a profit. Especially so, with an unknown playwright, who admittedly was supported by Arthur Milsop, thank goodness. At least he was somebody people might have heard of.

And then there was Dame Amelia, of course. But would anyone remember her after all these years?

-oOo-

Sir Philip and Lady Marchmont-Bone were already deep in discussion with agents and promoters about casting the show and the news that Herb and Amelia wanted to use it as a vehicle to try out some new talent came as no surprise to them. They had been having similar thoughts themselves.

They had managed to tactfully deflect Darren Beamish's entreaties to find a role for the talentless Alice Peabody, although Arthur Milsop's proposals to work his clumsy son into some minor part were less easy to discourage.

Arthur was at least working hard on the script and had circulated three corrected and revised sections for comment before the end of the week. Ira Samuels and Herb Walters met almost daily to review their cost estimates and plan the initial promotions for the show, and things were moving along nicely.

Dame Amelia watched over it all with a benevolent smile. She knew her lines and those of most of the other actors and she was ready to start work, but until the auditions began, there was little for her to do.

She tried to show some interest in other things going on around her, such as the sketches her daughter Camilla kept thrusting under her nose which related to the interior design of some castle in Scotland, but whilst she appreciated their artistry, she found it hard to concentrate on anything other than the play.

-oOo-

As the cocktails were handed round in the elegant drawing room of his London flat, Sir Philip took a folded piece of paper from his pocket.

'If you will indulge me, for a moment, I believe I have completed the draft cast list.' he said. 'If everyone is happy with it we can arrange for auditions to take place in the next couple of weeks.'

'Good,' said Arthur Milsop, taking a sip of his drink.

'I take it you found a role for my step-son, as we agreed?'

'Yes, Arthur. I have a role for Samuel, although all this is very provisional at present, of course.'

-oOo-

Chapter 35

The Play is the the Thing

'So, what is this play all about?' asked Annie, when she and Camilla were alone in the kitchen, back at the flat.

'I'll tell you in a minute. Will Hamish be all right while we go shopping, Annie?' asked Camilla, stepping into her shoes.

'Och! Will you look at him, there in that armchair! He is asleep already. He will be fine.'

'So he is,' observed Camilla, quietly closing the lounge door. 'You did tell him we were popping out …'

'Yes. He'll no stir 'till we get back, I'll wager.'

'Bless him. He looks very contented there.'

'I think he may be a wee bit tired, Milly. You see we

stopped at a hotel to break the journey, and ... well ...'

'Thank you, I can do without the pictures,' smiled Camilla. 'I'm very jealous, though ...'

'What? You would like to ...'

'Oh, I don't mean you and Hamish ... I mean Dicky ...'

'Ah, so you haven't ...'

'No.'

'But I thought ...'

'No.'

'Not even ...'

'No, not even then. Dicky is an absolute darling and a perfect gentleman,' said Camilla, closing the front door quietly behind them.

'Surely you want to ...'

'Oh God, yes. But the opportunity ... and if I'm honest I don't really know where to start ...'

'Well everybody is doing it. It is 1963, you know ... Oh, hang on, I think I get it. Is Dicky the first?'

'Not yet, but I hope he will be.'

In the of privacy of the little lift as it took them down to the ground floor, Camilla had a question.

'Annie …'

'Yes, Milly?'

'Um … What's it like, and what do you have to do?'

-oOo-

When Dicky got home from work, as Hamish and Annie had arrived at Camilla's flat she was anxious to bring them all together.

It was decided that Camilla and Annie would cook a meal, while Dicky and Hamish went for a beer at the local pub.

'Be back at eight, or I'm eating yours,' warned Camilla; and at a quarter to nine the boys rolled in and they all sat down to eat.

Camilla's succulent beef casserole with dumplings and vegetables was well received.

'This is delicious,' said Dicky.

'Mmmm!' added Hamish.

'All Camilla's work actually,' said Annie.

'Well, I don't very often get the chance to cook, and as this can be all prepared in advance and just goes in the oven, it is ideal for boys who don't know the difference between eight o'clock and ten to nine!'

'Sorry,' said Dicky between mouthfuls of the tasty

meal.

'Aye, me too,' added Hamish.

'By the way, feel free to use my car while you are here tomorrow,' said Dicky. 'I don't know what Jarvis did to it down at Holme Hall, but it is running really sweetly now. I'll leave you the keys.'

'Thanks, Dicky,' said Hamish 'That will make it easier tae get tae see all these caravans in this place somewhere off the North Circular Road, in the morning.'

'Yes, and the A-Z map book is in the car, if it helps.'

'Thanks, Dicky,' said Annie. 'That *will* help.'

-oOo-

And the map book did indeed help. They arrived at the caravan sales site with only one stop to consult the map, and ready to do business.

'Good Morning!' said John Cohen as they pulled into the yard behind the sign stating that this was "North Circular Caravans and Camping Supplies". 'Found us all right then?'

'Nae problem,' said Hamish. 'Nice ta see y'again, John.'

'Likewise, I'm sure, Hamish,' said the wiry little man who greeted them.
He drank in Annie and said 'and who do we have

here?'

'John, meet Annie, ma … ma, ay um, gurrl-friend.'

'How do you do!' said John, continuing to leer.

'Glad to meet you,' said Annie, with a pinched smile. 'Are the caravans this way?'

'Er, yes. That's right sweetie. The Eccles Alerts we discussed are in a row on the right, like.'

Annie slipped her hand through Hamish's arm as they approached the row of caravans.

'They are cute, Hamish,' she whispered. 'A wee bit old fashioned mebbe, but they do have a certain charm. I'm sure we could make them look lovely, with the right livery.'

Hamish knew he was in for an expensive morning.

-o0o-

'And if we paint the all caravans up so they match the best two,' said Annie, as they stood looking at the little collection they had chosen, some time later. 'We can make them all look very smart.'

'Aye,' said Hamish.

'Of course we are going to need quite a bit more Campbell Dress Modern clan tartan cloth,' Annie stated.

'Eh? What for?'

'To re-cover the seats and beds in all these caravans, of course. Then they will match the theme of the entire site.'

'Oh, no,' said Hamish. 'Does that mean we have tae trail round all those places again?'

'Och, no, Hamish! We only need tae visit the one we chose to supply the rest, to increase the order, when I've worked out how much we need.'

'Thank God!' said Hamish.

'It won't take me long to measure-up,' Annie was saying.

'Well, perhaps while you do that, I could take Hamish here into the office and we could discuss the money side of things, and delivery, and what have you,' said John, licking his lips.

'We'll need ta come back tomorrow with the money,' Hamish was saying, 'Assuming we can come to an arrangement on the price, of course …'

'Of course,' said John. 'Come on, I'll get the kettle on while your young lady gets her tape measure out.'

-oOo-

'So tell me what this play is all about, Camilla,' said Annie as they started on the washing up after dinner, and after Hamish and Dicky had gone through to the lounge.

'It is very funny in parts and has a clever plot involving the discovery of some sunken treasure just off the English coast.'

'And what part does your mother play?'

'She plays the hero's mother, and is a very grand Lady of the old school who bosses her children about unmercifully and interferes in their lives all the time.'

'I see.'

'Yes, so not much acting for mummy to do there then, just being herself.'

'Milly!'

'No, seriously, she has some cracking lines in this role and makes cutting remarks and spiteful comments whenever Pip, the hero, brings up the subject of getting the treasure up from the sea.'

'Does he get the treasure in the end?'

'Well, that is the clever bit. You see Pip is mummy's ... I mean Lady Celia Snook's second son and is renowned for coming up with silly money making schemes which fall flat on their faces. It is set in the 1920's and back then the first born son got to inherit and the second and subsequent sons had to work for a living.'

'Does he have a job, then?'

'Well no, and he is trying to avoid having to go to work in his wicked old Uncle's publishing company. Hence all the money making schemes.'

'So what happens?'

'Well, you see, this Pip has a bunch of ne'er-do-well chums who he meets up with in his London club. They are all in pretty much the same boat as he is. That seemed to be a common thing in the upper classes in the 1920's, and they all need money.'

'Are they a bunch of chinless public school boys?'

'Why, yes they are, as a matter of fact.'

'I thought so, I've read several stories like that.'

'Well, come to think of it, so have I, but this one goes off in a different direction.'

'With the discovery of the sunken treasure, you mean?'

'In a way, yes. You see Pip has been trying to curry favour with the sickly old father of the girl he is in love with, by reading to him in the evenings and listening to his reminiscences of his life with the old tea shipping companies out in India.'

'That sounds dull.'

'Deadly. Until the old boy suddenly decides he is dying, which he is of course, and he tells Pip about a sunken ship just off the English coast which was carrying back the possessions and ill-gotten gains of one of the tea plantation owners from the East India Company. This old boy had been collecting up and pinching all sorts of gold and silver objet d'art and so on, and the boat he was shipping it home to his family on sunk. Given the dubious nature of how he acquired some of this stuff, his family had not owned up to expecting it, and only the shipping company knew about it.'

'And the girl's dad tells him where it is?'

'With his last breath, and Pip then tries and mostly fails to raise the funds to launch a salvage mission.'

'Which he hopes will net him enough wealth to set him up, so he doesn't have to go and work for his wicked old uncle.'

'Well, yes. That's about it. But if you say it like that, it sounds a bit flat and predictable, but it actually bounces along and is full of all sorts of funny twists and turns.'

'And do they ever find the treasure?'

'Well, I don't want to spoil it for you, so you will have to buy tickets and go to the play to find that out,' laughed Camilla.

-oOo-

Hamish and Annie were still out in the little A30, concluding their business, when Dicky got home from work the next day.

He met Camilla coming in from the garden where she had been fussing Sid and feeding him his supper. Tonight that included some morsels of the beef casserole, which, she reported, were very well received.

'I'm not surprised,' said Dicky. 'It was a smashing meal, and if invited, I would have finished up those leftovers myself.'

'Well Sid got there first, I'm afraid. However, there is a little more left in the fridge, if you would like it.'

'Rather!' said Dicky, and followed Camilla into her flat.

-oOo-

It was some hours later when Annie turned the spare key in the front door of Camilla's flat. They had stopped for something to eat after concluding their protracted negotiations to buy a series of caravans, arrange delivery, and purchase cloth and various decorative items to make them stylish enough for their customers to use.

Although the sun had set and they had driven back with the headlights on, Annie was surprised to see that all the lights were off in the flat, and she was just about to call out to see if anyone was home, when Hamish shushed her and pointed at the closed door of Camilla's bedroom and the trail of clothes which led to it.

Hamish and Annie decided it was not too late to slip down to the pub.

-oOo-

Chapter 36

One year later

'You'll like this one,' said Camilla, passing Dicky a copy of the latest edition of 'Scottish Field' magazine. 'Great photographs of the castle.'

Dicky moved Sid the cat off his lap and took the magazine.

"Society joint wedding reception at Swinney Castle" proclaimed the headline, and Dicky read on into the text below the photographs.

"In early May, Swinney Castle hosted twin wedding receptions. Firstly of Hamish Swinney, Laird of the Swinney Estate, and Ann Mary Campbell-Manners, granddaughter of the celebrated Scottish architect, Douglas Campbell-Manners. The reception was combined with that of Richard James Bourne, playwright, and Camilla Jane Eloise Barron-Zukor;

only daughter of the famous Hollywood film and theatre actress, Dame Amelia Barron-Zukor. But the celebration showcased much more than the drawing together of these couples, and their lives have been intertwined for some time.

"Dame Amelia, who will be remembered for her velvet voice and charming performances in plays and films on both sides of the Atlantic, now stars in the highly- thought-of play *'Sunken Treasure'*, written by Richard Bourne and currently completing a two-week run at the King's Theatre in Edinburgh, before moving to the Apollo Theatre in London's West End (see review below). The scenery for the stage show was designed by Ann (Annie) Campbell-Manners, who is also a director of the company which runs the up-market game shooting, fishing and leisure complex at Swinney Castle.

"And the links don't end there: Camilla Barron-Zukor and Annie Campbell-Manners are old university friends, whereas Hamish Swinney and Richard Bourne met whilst on National Service in Germany, and Bourne and Camilla Barron-Zukor met when the latter's Bentley crashed into the former's car! Now Bourne's play, *'Sunken Treasure'* is gathering appreciative reviews, and it is rumoured, is about to be made into a film by Australian Director, Darren Beamish.

"The review below was first printed in 'Theatre and Cinema News, incorporating Box Office Magazine' and is reproduced by kind permission of Capt. E. Wilson, Managing Editor of that periodical.

"*Sunken Treasure* - A triumph from start to finish. The play, written by Richard Bourne with additional material by Arthur Milsop (Generation, Crisis Ahead, Train Ticket to Nowhere, etc.,) directed and produced by Sir Herbert Walters, is set to storm the West End after a successful run in provincial theatres.

"Introducing David Leslie, as Pip Ballatyne and starring Dame Amelia Barron-Zukor as Lady Celia Snook, the play amuses, captivates and charms in equal measure.

"With the haunting theme music by contemporary pop band Heather and the Heartaches and additional music provided by The Grinders (a versatile quartet of musicians from Scotland), set against sumptuous scenery designed by newcomer Annie Campell-Manners, of whom we expect to hear more, the lighthearted but involving action takes place in the elegant drawing-rooms and clubs of the 1920s.

"We are treated once again to the creamy smooth voice of Dame Amelia Barron-Zukor, lost to the world of theatre for too long, but now delivering sparkling dialogue as the irascible and scheming, but deceptively charming, Lady Celia Snook. The play could have been written for her, and her performance is a tour-de-force.

"The lead role is taken by a new, fresh face, in

the form of David Leslie. He holds the audience spellbound with his portrayal of the hapless Pip, who having discovered that an ancient treasure from India lies just beneath the waves, off the coast of Cornwall, struggles to find backers to go and find it. David Leslie is a name to watch. It may be some time before he needs to take on a different role, however, and he copes with his often-demanding dialogue with consummate ease and considerable aplomb. We expect this show to run and run.

"It is a rarity indeed when critics find nothing to complain about in a new show, but, apart from one unfortunate incident on the night of our review, where Samuel Milsop-Bishop, one of the minor players, tripped over the leg of a chair and measured his length on the stage and is no longer with the cast, we have nothing to criticise here and would urge readers to go and see this show. It will not disappoint."

'Oh, look,' said Dicky, returning the magazine to his wife, 'They have caught Sergeant and Mrs Ernest Bacon dancing in one of the photos.'

'Your favourite traffic warden loved his week away in one of Hamish's luxury caravans, didn't he,' smiled Camilla.

'Well, we old soldiers do have to stick together, you know,' said Dicky.

===
====

**The author will make a contribution
to The Royal British Legion
from the net profits of this book.**

Author's note:

This story is set in 1963 and although it is a work of fiction, whilst some names have been changed, all the historical context and references are accurate, as far as I have been able to reasonably establish.

Will future Governments have to resort to this tactic again to bolster our forces and provide front line soldiers? Or will they decide to use a refreshed form of National Service to refocus the anger and discontent we see today in so many young people?

I never imagined that I would speak out in favour of National Service, but recent events on the streets of the UK, fuelled by social media, may be turning me into *that* sort of a curmudgeon. Maybe that disciplined approach and roadmap on how to behave could work again, and turn out people with respect for each other. After all, if you teach a man to fight that is one thing, but if he knows that all his fellow men can also fight, it might give him second thoughts about starting a fight in the first place.

The National Army Museum has this to say about National Service:-
"The experience many men had of being thrown into combat situations, such as in Korea, Malaya and Suez, would never be forgotten. Men with minimal training were expected to fight guerrillas or cope with riots or civil war situations.
Between 1947 and 1963, a total of 395 National Servicemen were killed on active service."

By 1963 the British people generally were able to put the effects of the war behind them, and a great spirit of optimism emerged. Life was improving for ordinary people as well as the more privileged in all sorts of ways, and I hope I have highlighted some of the changes happening in that exciting era in this story. Things were improving on many levels. For example, although it was only a small thing, motorcars were being built with flashing indicators, front and back, rather than the quaint "trafficators", also called 'semaphore indicators', which were little illuminated arrows that popped out of the sides of the previous generation of cars, like Dicky's Austin A30. I'm sure that was a very positive improvement to road safety in itself!

Perhaps I should also explain that Adolf Zukor was the founder of Paramount Pictures. He emigrated to

America from Hungary in 1891 aged sixteen and started work as a furrier. He had one son named Eugene but, for the purposes of this story, I have invented another son, whom I've called Aaron, who married, and then divorced, the also fictitious Dame Amelia. That was long before she was a Dame, and was just plain Molly Pickering, a furrier's daughter from Bermondsey, London. She decided to continue to use the name 'Zukor' because she thought it was exotic and might help her in her career as a starlet in the world of motion pictures. Who can blame her? I imagined that her father-in-law, by then a successful film maker, had signed her up to Paramount before the ink was dry on the wedding certificate.

If you enjoyed this story and would like to discover more of my books, please enter 'Bob Able books' on Google or Amazon, and a link to my profile should appear.
If you liked this book please do leave a review on Amazon or Goodreads; you might be surprised at how much difference that really does make to bringing books to people's attention.

Cover Photo credit: Malcolma

Disclaimer:
Note: All rights reserved. No part of this book, ebook or manuscript or associated published or unpublished works

may be copied, reproduced or transmitted by any means, electronic, mechanical, photocopying or otherwise, without the prior written permission of the author.

Copyright: Bob Able 2024

The author asserts the moral right under the Copyright, Design and Patents Act 1988 to be identified as the author of this work.

This is a work of fiction, Any similarities between any persons, living or dead, except where noted, and the characters in this work is purely co-incidental.
The author accepts no claims in relation to this work.

About the Author:

Bob Able is a best selling writer of popular memoirs, fiction and thrillers. He describes himself as a 'part-time ex-pat' splitting his time between his homes in coastal Spain and 'darkest Norfolk' in the UK.

His memoir **'Spain Tomorrow'** was rated as the third most popular travel book by Amazon in September 2020 and with hundreds of reviews, continues to top the charts. With the sequel 'More Spain Tomorrow', followed by 'Third Helpings of Spain Tomorrow', these charming lighthearted insights into his life continue to amuse readers.

All his books are available as ebooks and paperbacks and can be found by entering 'Bob Able books' in the search bar.

If you like Bob Able's distinctive writing style and would like to read more of his work, here is a little more information.....
Stop Press! *Enter 'Bob Able books' on Amazon for details! ....*

'Poo, Power and Politics' now published as an ebook and a paperback

'Sarah's Kitchen' now published as an ebook and a paperback *See below!*

Bob Able writes with a lighthearted touch and does not use graphic descriptions of sex or violence in his books; that is not his style. He prefers to leave that sort of thing to the reader's imagination.

He has also produced a new series of lighthearted thrillers which will amuse as well as captivate readers. They are ideal light reads to take on holiday. The **Bobby Bassington Stories** include:
'Bobbie And The Spanish Chap',
'Bobbie And The Crime-Fighting Auntie',
'Bobbie And The Wine Trouble'
And **'Auntie Caroline's Last Case'**

All these books can be read on their own, although if you read them as a series, 'Auntie Caroline's Last Case' draws all the strings together and completes the tales of the lives of the characters we meet along the way.
Early reviewers had suggested that these stories would make an engaging TV series and of course Bob would be pleased to hear from television companies and promoters to explore that option!

His fictional novels include:
 'Double Life Insurance' a fast-moving but lighthearted thriller, where Bobbie Bassington first makes an appearance, fresh out of university:
'No Point Running' which is set in the world of horse racing and car theft in the 1970's before mobile phones and the internet:
'The Menace Of Blood', which is about inheritance, not gore, and the sequel
'No Legacy of Blood'.
They are all engaging thrillers, with a touch of romance and

still with that gentle, signature Bob Able humour.

His semi-fictional memoir **'Silke The Cat, My Story'**, written with his friend and wine merchant, Graham Austin and Silke the Cat herself, is completely different. Silke is a real cat, she lives today in the Costa Blanca, and her travels, which she recounts in this amusing book, really happened (also available as an audio book).

Contact:

bobable693@gmail.com
This is a 'live email address' and is monitored by Bob himself, so do not expect automated replies … Bob hates that sort of impersonal thing.

You can find details of how to buy all Bob's books and also follow him at:
www.amazon.com/author/bobable

Or just enter **'Bob Able books'** on the Amazon site or Google and the full list should appear.

Thank you for reading!

===========================

Here is an extract from one of Bob Able's latest books, 'Sarah's Kitchen', published in 2024. It would be a great holiday read and is available as an ebook or a paperback on Amazon.

Sarah's Kitchen

by Bob Able

Chapter 1

Originally she had set out to become a rocket scientist, of course, but that soon gave way to a plan to become a vet, then a nurse, and then, taking her brother's lead, she declared an interest in a life as a lady train driver.

Inevitably that didn't last, and now, several years after she had left school behind her, and most recently following many months as one of the growing army of unemployed single mums on the estate, Sarah was struggling to find a way to improve her lot.

She had always been a proficient and quite inventive cook, and became clever with pastry and cakes. But, as she never found a job which enabled her to use those skills, baking remained a hobby. Finances dictated that more recently she had to follow her mother's methods to produce food for the family. Those one- pot casseroles and quick pasta meals were fine when she and Ricky both had jobs, and even served well enough after Emma was born. But fancy cakes were a thing of the past.

Now, though, with Ricky gone to live with his barmaid, the pneumatic Stella; Emma at primary school and growing fast; and the job, that they promised they would keep open for her, vanished; her finances were increasingly a worry. So of necessity food became fuel, rather than fun.

When they got the house everybody on the estate had jobs, and most had two cars. Things looked rosy and the future was exciting. But then it all changed.

The Government said it was not just a problem for Great Britain, the recession which followed the financial crash was worldwide. It certainly seemed to leave almost nobody untouched on the estate. Ricky was one of the dozens who lost their jobs when the factory closed down, even though he was on a management training programme.

He got a better redundancy payment than some of their neighbours because of that, but he started spending it in the pub, and after a while he seemed to stop looking for work altogether.

That led to the rows, of course. And that led to the emergence of Stella, the landlord's niece. And that explained what Ricky was doing all day after Stella's shift finished at the pub.

Now it was just her and Emma. They still lived on the estate, but now they rented one of the flats over the little parade of shops.

At least it was cheaper than the mortgage she and Ricky had on the house, but when it was sold, there was only just enough money for the deposit on the rented flat left, after all the bills were paid. Although it was embarrassing, she was forced to 'sign-on' for Universal Credit.

There were six shops of varying sizes on the ground floor of the building, although only three were currently occupied.

The launderette was still open, and so was the wine merchant. But the hairdressers, the little supermarket and the newsagent had all long since closed down and been boarded up.

The last shop at the end of the parade had variously been a wine bar, an estate agents, a junk shop and a charity shop in the recent past, but now, after a long period sitting empty, it was being done up.

The builders said a slightly leery 'good morning' as Sarah passed by each day after walking Emma to school and she wondered what they were doing. Obviously she would not have had the courage to ask, however, were it not for the accident.

On that fateful day, as she rounded the corner on the way back from the school, and the shop came into view, a truck was parked unloading some building materials outside. One of the builders, who it later emerged was called Dave, was standing in the back of the truck throwing long metal scaffold poles over the side onto an untidy heap on the pavement. As she approached one of the poles landed on its end and sprang back, catching Dave on the side of his head and causing him to fall backwards from the truck, into the road.

Sarah rushed to help. She remembered some of the first aid course she did at work not long after Emma was born, and was able to stem the bleeding. Then she helped Pete, the other builder, to make Dave more comfortable until the ambulance arrived.

He was conscious but a bit dazed and while they sat with him on the road, Sarah asked what they were doing to the shop.

'It's going to be a cafe and a cake shop, I think,' said Pete. 'Although I can't see it doing any good round here unless they are planning to make it a greasy spoon, selling breakfasts or something.'

'Nah,' said Dave, coming to the surface. 'Amanda thinks she is going to make it a bakery type of thing, serving afternoon tea and what-not. Daft cow.'

'Amanda?' said Sarah, interested.

'Yeah. They are all like that up on Barclay Woods. Got some idea that this area is gonna be done up and ... what was that word she used, Pete?'

'Gentrified, Dave. Ah, here comes the ambulance.'

As the ambulance departed, Pete was finishing a call on his mobile phone.

'Derek is coming up to give me a hand to get this stuff off the pavement, although I shan't be able to do much more today on my own.'

'Derek?'

'Amanda's husband. He's Albany Developments. They've been buying up houses that have been re-possessed round here and doing them up.'

'Well, that's interesting,' said Sarah. 'I knew there were quite a lot of empty ones and there had been problems with them being vandalised. It will be good if they are being done up.'

'I think he is going to tart some of them up to rent out. He has got some deal on with the Council and a housing association, I think.'

'We bought one of the houses here when it was new. It was nice round here then,' said Sarah.

'Was it? Well, perhaps it will be again one day. Derek is planning to knock some of the houses down, build new ones for sale, and do up some of the others to rent. Have you seen that leaflet he was having delivered?'

'No. What leaflet?'

'Oh, you live in the flats, don't you, so you probably wouldn't have got one. The leaflet is asking if people who own houses here want to sell, and saying the area is going to be a regeneration project or something.'

'What? Knocking all the houses down?'

'Not all of them, I don't think. Only the ones built out of plywood; the timber frame ones with the funny roofs. There is a lot of them empty.'

'The council built them and then sold them off to some housing company. They always had problems with those odd looking steep roofs and damp getting in, especially after the original windows got replaced. I knew a couple of people who lived in them with mould growing up the walls who were desperate to get re-housed.'

'Well, those ones are nearly are all empty now and Derek's idea is to demolish them. But some of the other ones, the private ones, are rented out now and getting in a right old state, so Derek wants to knock some down and do others up for sale.'

'There have been problems with some of the people renting round there, I know. There are a couple of burnt-out cars up on the green, and the swing park is fenced off because it has been vandalised.'

'Dave told me the rumour is that there is some shady Indian or Pakistani bloke renting some of those houses out to asylum seekers and folk that even the council don't want to house. There was a drug dealer arrested ...'

'Yes, that was on the local news. There are stories like that all the time. I wish I could get my Emma away from here. I don't want her growing up amongst all that.'

'I know what you mean, love. But I guess unless your fella gets a better job somewhere else ...'

'Unfortunately he got what he considered a better opportunity somewhere else some time ago, and it's just Emma and me now.'

'I'm sorry ... I'm Pete, by the way.'

'Sarah,' said Sarah. 'Is this Derek coming now, in that big Mercedes?'

-ooo0oo-

Sarah had had a cleaning job for a short while, up on Barclay Woods, working for a company that cleaned several of the posh houses up there.

She hoped to get Ricky a temporary job being advertised for a gardener in one of the big houses on that estate, but he wouldn't hear of it. He was a qualified engineer, he said, and was almost management trained. He considered a gardening job was beneath his dignity.

Sarah failed to get Ricky to accept that the type of engineering work he could do was history, and he would simply *have* to retrain to get another job. His answer to that was to create a job for himself propping up the bar in Stella's pub.

Sarah liked the large houses on Barclay Woods and enjoyed cleaning them with the jolly crew of girls she worked with. It was a pity that the company folded, and that the efforts a couple of the girls made to take over the cleaning round didn't work out.

The difference between the lives the Barclay Woods residents enjoyed and those endured by the residents of her estate could not be more marked, and Sarah often wondered how they did it.

-ooOOoo-

'How's Dave?' called Sarah as she passed Pete working on the scaffolding outside the shop a few days later.

'Hi, Sarah. Concussion. Been given ten days off, lucky bleeder!'

Hearing the talking outside, Derek emerged from the interior of the shop.

'Ah ha! Are you Sarah?' he asked, 'Can I thank you for helping Dave when he had his little accident. It was very kind.'

Sarah blushed and could not immediately think of anything to say. She thought what she did was only what anyone would do in the circumstances.

'He's got to stay at home and take it easy for a while, but after the hospital stitched him up he was laughing and joking with the nurses in no time. Typical Dave, that is. Suzanne, Amanda's sister calls him the life and soul, looking for a party.'

Sarah smiled at the little joke.

'I'm Derek, by the way. Dave is my brother-in-law,' and he held his hand out for Sarah to shake.

'How do you do,' said Sarah coyly.

'Pete tells me you live in the flats up there,' Derek was saying. 'You are probably wondering what this shop is going to be and what we are doing with it ...'

'Well, I ...'

'It is Amanda's pet project. And what Amanda wants, she gets, if you know what I mean. Amanda, my wife, has a vision to turn this into an artisan bakery and tea shop. She has all sorts of plans drawn up and swatches and what-have-you prepared for the wallpaper and the fabrics covering the chairs and so on; all themed with her latest favourite. Hares. It is going to be called the Mad Hatter's Tea Rooms, she informs me, although until I can get the regeneration of this grotty old estate up and running, she is the mad one if you ask me!'

'It was once very nice round here,' said Sarah.

'Oh. Sorry, no offence meant, but you have to admit it is long overdue for a spruce up. When I've finished with it, it will be very pleasant again, I hope. And a desirable place to live.'

'Is he laying out the grand vision for Albany Developments world dominance again?' smiled Pete, climbing down from the scaffolding. 'And I thought he was just here to make the tea.'

-ooOOoo-

For a change Emma ate up all her tea without a complaint. The cottage pie Sarah had made met with her approval, and she even finished up the peas.

'What are they doing to that shop downstairs, mummy?' she asked between mouthfuls, and Sarah explained Amanda and Derek's plans. 'We went to a tea shop like that once didn't we, mummy. I think it would be nice.'

Emma was referring to a trip they had taken a year ago to see Sarah's brother, Emma's uncle Matthew, who lived in leafy Surrey, near Dorking. The trip was still green in her memory and Emma adored her uncle and his industrious wife, Sandy, who ran her own little business from home making teddy bears. Emma's most prized possession was one of those bears, which when not involved in imaginary picnics and other games was always within reach, and accompanied her to bed every night.

Matthew was doing well, and since college had a job in the Local Council where he seemed to work in the office on something mysterious to do with trees. When Sarah and Ricky had split up he had helped with selling the house and dealing with the solicitors, and then finding Sarah and Emma the flat where they now lived.

With no children of their own, Matthew and Sandy spoilt Emma and could always be relied upon for the more expensive sort of Christmas and birthday presents. Emma did not know it, of course, but there had been conversations about getting her a bicycle for her next birthday in six weeks time. Sarah was very grateful to them and certainly could not contemplate buying such extravagant presents herself.

But there was a problem. If Emma had a bike, where could she ride it safely? There was no way that Sarah could let her ride it around the estate, that was simply out of the question. And riding it to school meant a main road which was much too busy for children cycling. Sarah did not want to disappoint Emma or frustrate her need to spread her wings on a bike, and she remembered the joy she felt when she was given her first bicycle. But that was down in the quiet lanes near Dorking, where she grew up, not in the run-down sprawl where they lived now.

Not for the first time Sarah regretted following Ricky to the inner suburbs and his work in the factory. The whole thing seemed like a golden dream back then, but over time it had turned into a depressing grinding disappointment, and now it looked as though there was no way out.

Chapter 2

When she was two, Sarah's father bought a victorian 'villa' in the village of Westcott, on the outskirts of Dorking from where he could take the longish walk, or more usually cycle, to the railway station, and on to his work in the City of London.

She attended the local school, following two years behind her brother, and they rode their bikes alongside Pipp's Brook and through Squire's Wood; where, in a pool near the source of the brook, they swam as children.

There were picnics in the fields and trips for walks on Ranmore Common, and on summer weekends as she grew, her parents would occasionally take her to the Prince of Wales pub for lunch, a few doors along from the ramshackle cycle shop that provided her first and much treasured bicycle.

As she grew, she joined the 'Young Farmers Association', and that is how she met Ricky.
The Young Farmers organised trips to farms, obviously, but also to places connected with the business of farming, including, one hot summer day, to the County Show, in Guildford.

As a group they visited the various manufacturers of agricultural implements and machinery displaying their wares at the show. There Sarah met Ricky, an apprentice sent down with the company representatives to keep the Rectangular Balers and Conveyors they manufactured, and were displaying with a tractor to pull them, clean and shiny to impress the visitors and potential buyers.

When she first saw him, Ricky was working in the baking sun standing high up on the deck by the steering wheel of the tractor, polishing invisible specs of dust from the paintwork, with his shirt off. Having just turned sixteen and still quite impressionable, Sarah was instantly smitten.

Although slim and yet to develop what you might call a muscly torso, nineteen year old Ricky already had a broad chest and cut quite a striking figure in tight fitting and highly fashionable 'camouflage trousers' and rigger boots. Sarah was very impressed and became all the more-so when, now with his shirt on, he joined the young farmers in the beer tent and bought her a half pint of cider.

As the leader of their group was gathering the young farmers up by the minibus which was collecting them, Ricky and Sarah shared their first brief kiss and Sarah could not resist resting her hand on his impressive chest under his unbuttoned shirt. As they fixed up their first date, Sarah was already under Ricky's spell.

Given Sarah's age, her parents were naturally concerned that she should not spend too much time with Ricky and imposed strict curfews and deadlines to limit the time they spent together. But five weeks later, after they gave permission for a trip in Ricky's elderly car to the nearby cinema for a matinee performance; in a quiet country lane and in broad daylight, Sarah became a woman. They never made it to the cinema.

-ooOOoo-

When Pete and Derek mentioned that Dave was due back to work on Monday, as she passed by and enquired after his health, Sarah did something quite out of character, extravagant and potentially foolish. But she loved doing it and was pleased with the result.

Sarah baked a selection of fancy cakes to present to the builders, to celebrate Dave's return.

There were little individual upside down apricot and orange cakes, slices of almond, blueberry and vanilla cake, two different sorts of madeleines, and slices of indulgent creamy 'millefeuille' with layer after razor thin layer of puff pastry and creamy custard topped with a rich fondant icing, decorated with a web design in chocolate. Sarah couldn't really afford the ingredients for these extravagant cakes, but something drove her to revisit her old hobby, and she throughly enjoyed making them.

She knew that Derek, Pete and Dave stopped for coffee at ten o'clock, and she turned up with the tray of fancies under a tea-towel just at the right time.

'Where did you buy these?' asked Derek; and when Sarah admitted she had made them, he made Dave put his slice of cake, un-bitten, back on the tray and took a photograph on his mobile phone of the entire assemblage.

'You really made these?' asked Dave incredulously, as Pete, taking a bite of almond, blueberry and vanilla cake, let out a little sound of delight as the various flavours danced on his tongue.

'It's just a hobby,' blushed Sarah as the two builder's men heaped praise on her after each mouthful they took.

Derek however was quiet, and while he tasted, and clearly enjoyed the cakes, he passed no comment until they had nearly all gone.

'Sarah,' he said, 'it was extremely kind and generous of you to make those, especially for an undeserving work-shy pair like these two. How much do I owe you for the cakes?'

'Oh no!' said Sarah, taken aback. 'It is nothing like that. I did it for my own pleasure as much as anything else. I certainly wasn't looking to sell you anything.'

As she spoke Derek was wrapping the last of the cakes in the tea-towel.

'Is it all right if I get the tea-towel washed and give it back to you on Wednesday?' asked Derek. 'I want Amanda to try these!'

-ooO0oo-

Emma enjoyed the cakes too, and devoured the rest of the selection that Sarah had not taken to the builders with determination.

'Lovely, Mummy!' she said smacking her lips and wiping the last crumbs from her chin. 'When are you going to bake some more?'

Emma went to bed with a full tummy, telling 'Edward', her bear, all about the cakes and discussing with him the virtues of each one, in the order she ate them.

In the evening, as Sarah sat with the little book in which she tried to keep track of their finances and entered her expenditure for the week, she had to admit that it would be some time until she could afford another extravagant baking day like that. The rest of the month was going to be very tight. She had enjoyed doing it, but looking at the figures now, she had to face the facts and regretted her rash act.

As she stared at them, the figures in the little book began to dance before her eyes, and she found that she was crying.

-ooO0oo-

To discover how to read more, look for a link to 'Sarah's

BOB ABLE

Kitchen' at www.amazon.com/author/bobable

https://www.amazon.co.uk/stores/Bob-Able/author/B07VZBFFBZ

or https://tinyurl.com/yptuftnp

Printed in Great Britain
by Amazon

52061885R00182